Escaping
Tainted
Love

JESSICA CHIC

DEDICATION

Writing has always been a dream of mine ever since I was a little girl, and this book is my proof that dreams do come true. Some dreams need the love and support of family, friends and spouses to help carry them to the finish line. I would like to thank my best friend Tamiko for always pushing me to do better and reach my goals. To my friend Bryan for always supporting my dreams and goals like an encouragement of a pillar of strength in my corner. To my children for behaving in the most well-mannered way allowing mommy to write this book... I know it was hard! And most importantly to Josh for being the wind beneath my wings and the air in my lungs giving me the drive to push through all the struggles on getting this done. Thank you for putting so much work and effort and for being the man I need you to be, I love you. Without each and every important person in my support system, this book may have just remained a dream. I love you all!

DISCLAIMER

This book is a work of fiction. All locations real or fabricated are simply to set the scene for the reader. All characters and events are fictitious and any likeness or similarity is purely coincidence.

CONTENTS

FOREWORD

I woke up this morning with joy in my heart, gratitude on my lips and a curious thought as to how I am the very person I am today. What life events impacted me in such ways to get me to this very point in my life? I try to shake off the thought, "come on Gwen just let it go and move on with the day." I tell myself. Suddenly my mind starts to pull memories to the surface I thought I had buried, all the fear, loss, love, pain and joy I have lived start playing in my mind like and old black and white movie. As I approach my mirror in the bathroom, I see my post-it note telling myself to keep my thoughts positive and thank God for at least three things before I start my day. So, my mind quickly shifts from playing my old memories and I focus on the elements of happiness; I am thankful for my health and life, I am thankful for my wonderful husband and I am thankful for my beautiful children. Then as if I can't control my thoughts my mind circles around to wondering; how many people don't analyze their lives in wonderment of who they are, and how they became the person they are.

After I shower and apply my makeup, I feel beautiful I thank God for giving me the ability to enjoy the process of applying makeup; which feels like a mixture of art and therapy. Getting dressed always seems to be an O.C.D. ridden stressor for me, because I take pride in not only feeling beautiful but also staying trendy. Once I settle on a nice pair of true religion jeans, with a solid light blue tank and black feather duster with light blue floral print and my most comfortable black boots; I look in my mirror while putting my gun and holster belt on. I thank God once more for all my assets and blessings and I head out. As I start walking down the street I wonder, what made that man want to become a teacher, or that woman a police officer? I think about the truth in the fact of, no matter our background we all become who we are based on life choices and experiences. Whether you are a thief, rapist, murder, F.B.I., judge, teacher, doctor, gardener, nurse, store clerk or any other piece of the fabric of society, you got there by the experiences and choices that landed you right where you are. Suddenly, as my mind is running through all these thoughts I back track and wonder what kind of terrible experiences make someone a rapist or a murderer. I try to imagine what tragedies that weigh down and form a survivor to become someone who can't turn away from sharing their hurt. What is it that just pushed their mind over the edge? Then I remind myself that I know all too well from experience we have a choice. We can choose how we respond to life events and we can turn our lives around.

I am so thankful that I am the woman I am today; but I was not sure I would be at this point of gratitude and abundance before. So, I am thankful as I walk into my office and see my team of FBI agents I work with. I whisper a kind thank you to God and the universe for giving me another day to grow from experiences, perspective and choices. When I work a case I don't see it as all the bad or evil in the world, I see lost and broken people that haven't been able to see life from another perspective. I see a world full of people that have been conditioned by Hollywood to be negative and thrive on it.

So, I send out a prayer blessing the people around me who live off impulse and are drowning in their own pools of negativity.

So, what were all those impactful life experiences that made me who I am anyway? How long was I caught in the rip current of the narrow water that flows directly away from the shore, and is always threatening to drown me in negativity. How long did I spend blaming God for everything wrong in my life and not being thankful for what I did have?

To figure that out we are going to have to start from the beginning...

CHAPTER 1

THE NEW ADDITION

I am so excited today I get to meet my new baby brother! My daddy is coming to get me, "his little princess" and is taking me to the hospital to meet the new baby. I can't help but wonder why the baby is at the hospital, maybe he got sick or the stork dropped him on the way to our house. That can't be right because the stork carried baby Dumbo to his mommy just fine, I know because I saw it on tv myself! I am at Grandpa Alfred's and Grandma Sky's (she is half Cherokee and half Irish and has the most beautiful Sky-blue eyes hence her name,) I love sleeping over at their house. They get up really early at about 4:30 in the morning and I can smell the amazing scent of coffee being brewed and hear the sound of my grandpa's smokers cough. So, I get out of bed and sit in the chair to the left of my grandpa. I really love listening to grandpa's stories; I ask him to tell my favorite one about how the unicorns didn't want to get on the Ark with Noah because they wanted to play. After the story was done grandma gave me some cut up fruit and cottage cheese, my favorite breakfast! Then she gave me a bath and helped me get dressed; I loved the gentle way she had about her when she was helping me. Just then I could hear the roar of the Camaro engine and the blaring rock n' roll music that cuts off to a door slam, daddy was here. As daddy rushes in I can feel a nervous excitement as he comes in the door, "Princess?" " I'm here daddy, right here…"I say. Then I ask him where mommy is; he laughs a little and tells me she is at the hospital with the baby. Oh my gosh now mommy is sick? Or maybe she is just sitting with the baby! Yeah, that has to be it…!

Daddy scoops me up in his arms and I feel safe. His muscular arms around me are like the strongest safety net in the world, and the smell of Grey Flannel cologne surrounds me. He helps me into my car seat and then jumps in the front seat; he must be really excited because he seems to be in a rush. On the ride over I am so excited and I try to yell over the loud music to ask daddy if grandma and grandpa are going to see the baby too, but he can't hear me over the music. So, I settle back against my seat wishing that daddy wanted to listen to me as much as he wanted to listen to Led Zeppelin. Just then my favorite Led Zeppelin song comes on and I forget about that thought and start rocking out and singing along to Nobody's Fault but Mine. My daddy is really happy to see me singing along in the rear-view mirror and gives me a wink and a smile.

As we walk into the hospital, daddy picks me up and swings me up onto his shoulder, and tickles me too make me laugh as he carried me and walked to the gift shop. When we get into the gift shop daddy gently sets me down in front of the flowers. He is getting flowers for mommy, and says I can get something for my brother. Daddy can't decide which flowers to get for mommy, so he asks me if I like the lilies, I scrunch up my face and remind him that mommy hates lilies. The last time daddy got her lilies she complained that lilies smell like a funeral. Daddy laughed and said, "thank goodness little girls are born little women, they don't miss a thing!" So, he picks out an arrangement of red roses and pink Gerber daisies and they smell heavenly. Daddy said I could pick something special for my new baby brother and he gives me a five-dollar bill to hold, I am so excited. "I'm a big girl now with my own money." I said. I get to pick out something all by myself for my new baby brother. I just turned two last month… so… I know just how excited my brother will be to get my gift. I picked out a baby gorilla stuffed animal with a light blue shirt, a white and light blue polka dotted diaper and a real baby pacifier attached to it. When we arrive in the hospital room daddy lifts me up to see the baby, he is the cutest, smallest little person I have ever seen. Mommy says I can put the gorilla in his little baby bed as she sits on her bed and lifts me up to help me. Then mommy puts me in the bed with her. She is warm and smells like the Irish Spring soap she just used to shower before we got here. My mommy snuggles me in under her blankets with her on her hospital bed and sings Twinkle, Twinkle Little Star to me as I settle into her warm and loving embrace. I ask her what his name is, wondering what kind of name is perfect for a prince. She tells me his name is William Henry Collins, it's perfect, I didn't expect anything less. My parents gave me the perfect name for a princess, Guinevere Elizabeth Collins, but everyone calls me Gwen, unless I have been naughty….and I can always tell because mommy hollers my full name. I wonder if my brother will have a nickname name too.

With William and mommy back home, I couldn't be happier. Mommy and daddy let me help with the baby. I love holding him and looking at his little hands and feet. He smiles a big toothless smile whenever I talk to him and it is so cute. It's hard to be quiet when he is sleeping and mommy and daddy yell at me to be quiet, "shhhhhh Gwen you are being too loud!" "Shit the baby is awake now, I will never get him back down." I don't understand why they are yelling if we should be being quiet. How much sleep does a baby need anyway; he sure does sleep a lot. Mommy told me we are going to go play at the beach for a little while just me and her. I love the beach, I can't wait to breathe in the sea air and sunscreen. I love digging my toes into the sand, collecting sea shells and swimming in the ocean water. I learned to swim in the ocean and I am sure my brother will too because mommy and daddy like to surf. When I see that she walks out without the baby I burst into tears and stop following her. I dig in my heals and like word vomit demand, "Where is my baby?" "Your daddy is watching him so we can have a mommy daughter day sweetie," She says. "I don't want a mommy and daughter day without my baby," I say. Mommy lets out a little laugh, "Ok honey, we'll find something we can all do." She said and she brings me in for a big hug. I love mommy hugs, she smells so good like Coco Chanel perfume, and I always feel safe and warm in her hugs. We go back inside to collect baby Will to visit the park and mommy and daddy share a funny look with shrugs. Then mommy grabs Will's diaper bag and a light baby blanket so she can nurse him if she needs to and change his diapers if he needs freshening up. Daddy gathered my sand toys for mommy and we headed to the park to play.

William is seven months old and I love him but sometimes I wish mommy and daddy could play with me more. I also wish that Will. Would stop slobbering all over my toys. All I can do is watch in horror as his drool filled lips open revealing his two new teeth as he bites down on my stuffed Big Bird. Stuffed animals don't even taste good. I start to cry and yell for mommy to help me get my Big Bird away from Will. When she comes into the living room and sees me pulling on Big Bird she yells, "GUINEVERE ELIZABETH COLLINS YOU STOP PULLING THAT AWAY FROM THAT BABY RIGHT NOW!". Mommy tells me I need to learn to share but I don't see why, Will has his own toys, why can't he just keep his little hands on his own stuff?

I got in big trouble and was sent to my room to play quietly because daddy didn't like my language. I don't understand what a language is … and I did what I was told. He told me to think about my behavior, so I am! Daddy asked, "Gwen can you get me a diaper?" I told him, "Get your own damn diaper!" I was mad because I wanted a story but I had to play because he was taking care of Will. The look on his face told me I better get that diaper. So, I did and when I gave it to him and said, "here is your damn diaper!" He said thank you but then told me he didn't like my language and sent me to my room to think and play quietly. When mommy got up from her nap, daddy told her about what I had done and she laughed and told me not to say bad words. I told mommy that it wasn't fair that I couldn't say those words, because daddy said them every time, he was watching the 49er's games. I learned to expand my vocabulary with a sprinkle of choice words while watching those games with daddy, wearing his jersey shirt and jumping up every time the Niners scored. I would jump up and cheer that they made a home run. I don't know how words can be bad but I won't do that again. I better figure out the words that are bad because a princess should probably never use them. Mommy gives me a big hug and then scoops me up to carry me to the table for lunch, the smell of grilled cheese fills my nose. I probably should have stop laughing and playing at the table like mommy told me, because a bite of grilled cheese got stuck in my throat. Thank goodness my mommy was right there, she had to lay me on her knee and hit my back really hard until the piece of sandwich flew out. Mommy and daddy looked really scared while I was choking because I couldn't talk or breathe.

My mommy saved me.

CHAPTER 2

KIDNAPPERS

We all load into the car with bags, daddy says we have a long drive ahead of us. As we turn our new dark blue car onto the freeway, I ask where we are going and daddy says Victorville. I am not happy about being in the car for so long. So, after thirty minutes have passed, I start asking, "are we there yet?" But asking every two minutes was making daddy a little upset, so I rested my head on the side of my car seat and went to sleep."

 We are visiting my dad's birth family, he was adopted but has been trying to build a relationship with his birth mom. I don't know what all that means but I don't care too much for this "grandma" and I won't call her grandma because she isn't mine. So, I gladly call her nanna as she asks. I don't like her house either, she lives in what they call a trailer park and it is hot and dirty outside. Her house is up above the ground and she has plants on the porch, but I still don't like it. When we go in, I am hit with a smell that I don't like, it smells funny inside. I see my aunt Tracy as she is heading out to pick something up. Nanna is sitting on the couch with my daddy's other brothers and sisters, there are so many I don't take the time to remember all their names. When my cousin Jeremy comes into the room nanna throws her house slipper at him and tells him to go turn the tv off he left on. What a bitch, I really don't like nanna…she is one of the meanest people I have ever seen. Plus, she stinks, she smells like cigarettes and Bengay which really makes me want to cough and gag.

My daddy, his brothers and the other men are going to barbeque. Mom has to go to the store and asks nanna to keep an eye on me. When mom heads out to find a store in this nasty Victorville place we are visiting, I notice she forgot Will's favorite blanket. What if he gets cold or starts to cry, it is the only thing that with take care of those things. He is getting new teeth and mommy says all his crying is normal at his age, of nine months old. I scoop up the blanket and rush outside, I didn't have time to track down that terrible nanna and tell her. I have to get the blanket to mommy for Will. I start walking around the trailer park looking for mommy, but I can't find her. When I look around, I notice I must have wandered too far because now I am lost. I don't see nanna's trailer they all look the same. A wave of fear starts to swell inside me and tears start streaming down my face. I am so scared and I am calling out for mommy hoping I can find her or find my way back to the terrible funny smelling trailer. It is so hot and I am thirsty.

I feel like I have been looking for mommy for

such a long time, my feet hurt and I struggled to see through my tears while working to keep the baby blanket clean for Will. I sat down just for a second on the porch of a trailer I thought was nanna's, but the old man inside came out yelling at me to get off his porch. I was running so fast I didn't notice the car that was headed toward me. When I slowed down and looked up, I saw the car was in front of me. It is a very ugly red color. As it gets closer, I can see there are two people in the car. A man that has a ring of hair around his head, with a comb over and a large bushy mustache; and a woman that has long black stringy hair and huge glasses on. She isn't wearing any makeup like mommy does either. The car stops very close to me and I hear the man say "Make sure you grab her fast" as the woman opens the passenger side door and says, "Are you lost?" I stand there for what feels like ages, petrified with fear I can feel the pain in my feet yet I can't seem to move them as if they have turned to two heavy bricks. I can see that both of them are dressed in the ugliest outfits, but where have I seen those outfits. Yes, on the soldiers on tv, the army guys in the MASH show my daddy watches dress like that. They are also wearing big black combat boots with their ugly muddy green uniforms. They must be soldiers like the ones on tv. When I collect myself enough, I say, "I am looking for my mommy and baby." The lady gets out of the car and something about her makes me feel very afraid. She snatches me up and is trying to shove me in the car. The smell of her sweat and cigarettes engulfs my nose and I start to cry harder. I can see now through my tears that there is a large hand gun on the seat. I begin kicking and screaming for help hoping that someone, anyone can hear me. The mean lady is twisting and pulling my arm hard, up and behind my back and it hurts like nothing I have ever felt before. I am so afraid; why is this bitch trying to hurt me, where are they trying to take me, where is my mommy and daddy?

I am so afraid... I feel like my heart is beating in my tummy, I can feel my blood pulsing so fast through my body I can almost hear it. Just when I start to think there is no escape from this woman's clutches, my daddy's sister Tracy pulls up in her white car and I am thankful to see her here. She jumps out even though she just had knee surgery, and starts screaming at the lady, "Give me my niece, right now! What do you think you are doing?" The lady ignored my aunt and continued to still try to shove me into the car. I was kicking off the seat, back into her struggling and fighting, not allowing her to get me into the car. Somehow....I know that if she gets me into the car, I won't see mommy or daddy again. Aunt Tracy runs up, yanks the lady back and punches her in the face while yelling for help. People start coming out to see what all the commotion is and the lady lets me go into the embrace of my aunt. The lady jumps in the car and they speed off causing a huge amount of dirt to kick up into the air. I breathe in the smell of my auntie and her Loves Baby Soft perfume and allow myself to cry in the safety of her arms.

Back at the house my mommy is relieved to have me in her arms, and I glad to be in the safety of her embrace. She has tears in her eyes and can't stop kissing me and I can smell her perfume, the Coco Chanel smell reminds me of how much mommy's hugs mean to me. There are two police officers talking to my aunt to find out what happened and gather details. When they come over to talk to me, I am afraid that I am in trouble for wandering off, but I am not in any trouble. The officers ask me some questions about what I remember and then give me a lollipop. They tell me I am safe now and promise that they will find those bad kidnappers. Kidnappers is a new and strange word, but I never want any more of those bad people around me again. I am still really afraid and know that from now on I won't go anywhere without mommy or daddy. The world has suddenly become so big and scary to me.

CHAPTER 3

SCHOOL BEGINS

Time flies by so fast, and I love watching cartoons in the morning with Will in my lap. He is such a good little brother. Mom says I have to be to bed early because I am starting kindergarten tomorrow. I am excited and scared all at the same time; I am really a big girl now. I wonder if that is how dad felt when he started his new job at Boeing building airplanes.

We moved into a big two-story house in the Long Beach Country Club a few months ago. I have my very own room now on the second floor. It's pink and I have Lisa Frank posters on the walls. The rainbow-colored panda bear might just be my favorite. I got my hair trimmed yesterday and today I am going shopping with grandma and grandpa for new school clothes. They offered to take me because my brother can be quite a handful these days. He is two now and full of energy and just as much trouble. Yesterday he was climbing on the book shelf while mom was cleaning the kitchen; thank goodness she came to check on him because he really could have gotten hurt.

Mom is calling me which means grandma and grandpa are here to pick me up. I grab my sunglasses and put my Chapstick in my pocket, and head down stairs. As we head out, I can feel all this excitement building and soon we are at the mall. I get all kinds of clothes; shirts, pants, sweaters, skirts, shorts, and I even got a pair of new L.A. Gears. I am so happy; I can't wait to meet my new teacher tomorrow.

Mom was up early and made breakfast, the smell of sausage and eggs was all through the kitchen. When mom gave me my plate and poured me my orange juice, she told me that I wouldn't have time to watch more than two cartoons with Will this morning; we watched Scooby Doo first. It was always so funny how Shaggy talked to his dog and we both laughed every time Scooby got scared by the ghosts or monsters they were chasing. Then we watched Popeye; Will really loves to eat spinach because he wants to be big and strong like Popeye. When Bluto tries to steal Olive Oyl away from Popeye we always wonder if he is going to win, but thankfully he doesn't. When the cartoon episodes were finished, I brushed my teeth and put on the clothes mom laid out for me. I am glad I learned how to tie my shoes because I don't have to wait for mom to do it for me. Then mom brushes my long blonde hair and puts it half up in a hair tie that has two big pink balls on it. Then she walks me to school with Will in the stroller. On the way she tells me she is going to be going back to work soon and we will have a new babysitter.

Mom is a nurse so I am happy that she will be able to be back at work helping people. She works with a doctor that takes care of mommies that are waiting for their babies to be delivered. I wonder, how do the storks get the babies in the first place? What is the doctor for and why do the mommies need one? It makes me wonder exactly how the storks know which mommy and daddy belong to which baby. Where do they make the babies? It's all such a mystery; and one I am quickly distracted away from because I see a little kitty in the middle of a the very busy street we are crossing. He runs alongside us and mom scoops him up. He is so dirty, but she said she is going to take him home and clean him up. It was so, so exciting and now I can't wait to go home and see him later even though I haven't even started my day.

When we arrive at the school, I am a little more afraid than I am excited, it's so big and I don't know anybody. Mom has to leave me here, and that causes a growing anxiety to fester with flashes of my near kidnapping at two years old; I am four now but it doesn't feel like any time has passed, it is so burned into my mind. What if there are kidnappers at school, they are all strangers after all. Mom walks me into the classroom and it smells like crayons, paste and paint, I can even smell the paper there is so much of it. I meet my teacher, Mrs. Hall. She is very nice and welcomes me in, she smells sweet like watermelon and cucumber and she has a nice smile. She rings her bell and gathers all the kids into the classroom from the playground and we all sit on the floor with our legs crossed; Indian style they called it. The teacher tells us what we will be doing and all the fun we will have this year. It is all so exciting. When mom leaves, I feel a surge of panic wash over me and I can't tear my eyes away from the door. Suddenly I am hyper aware of all that is going on around me and I am keeping an eye out for anyone who might try to steal me away.

I just turned five and I got lots of new toys. I wonder if Will is going to get just as many for his birthday in two months. I am getting pretty good at keeping track of the days, weeks, and months now because of my teacher and her cool calendar. It's March which means the raining has stopped and we get more days to play outside at free time, it's so much fun jumping rope, or playing farm. We went on a field trip to a farm to see how the farmers work. When I got off the big yellow school bus the air was pungent with the smell of barn animals and their waste. I was so happy seeing the pigs, cows, horses and all the farming equipment. The turkeys on the other hand were down right terrifying. I touched one on the head; it looked like he had colorful corn on his head and I wanted to feel it. Wow was that a mistake he started chasing me and I was truly running for my life. If it wasn't for the farmer scooping me up, I am sure that turkey was going to really kill me, he was so mad.

After all the fun and learning I was doing this year in kindergarten I felt so proud and happy. I can read and write and for the first time ever, I know for sure I am a big girl now. Sometimes though I still make mistakes, I sure can't wait to be a grown up because they never seem to make mistakes. Clay and I got in trouble today because some of the other kids wanted us to kiss so we did; then they told on us. Boy Mrs. Hall was sure upset, she made us go to the behavior chart and find our names and hand her our green cards. I cried so hard, I had never had to lose my green card before and now as I sit looking at my yellow card I can't stop crying. I am not crying because I am sad, I am crying because I am mad, how dare Mrs. Hall tell me kissing is bad. I don't understand why kissing was so bad. It was just a quick peck on the lips and I see people do it all the time, even the ones on tv. It's ok anyway because the school year is almost over, I will make sure I stay out of trouble from now on. I hate being in trouble.

Daddy took me for a ride just to get out of the house and he let me sit in his lap to drive the car. Of course, I was not really driving daddy was helping me. Every time I saw a red car, I really wanted to crash into it. I hated red cars, and I would cry to daddy, "hit that red car daddy, please!" My daddy would just tell me that nobody ever wants two cars to crash because people could get hurt. I don't understand why he didn't know that red cars are the cars that belong to bad guys, like those awful kidnappers.

CHAPTER 4

CATHOLIC SCHOOL BLUES

I am so excited to be starting the third grade. Although I love my days spent at the beach soaking up the rays of the summer sun and smelling the salty beach water; I really miss and love my friends. After kindergarten, I started going to a Catholic school, Saint Athanasius. I wear uniforms for school now; they are blue plaid colored with solid white shirts. The boys wear navy blue pants with solid white shirts, I think because plaid pants might look a little silly. The girls can't wear nail polish which I hate, and we also can't wear makeup of any kind even though some of the older girls seem to get away with it. I really like that this school goes up to the eighth grade and we have big buddies. Having a big buddy system in place is fun and sometimes our big buddies help us with our homework or give us money for popsicles or school carnival tickets to play the games. I really am not looking forward to seeing Shelia, she is so mean. During our first communion last year, she had to stand behind me in line and she was jabbing in the back the whole time. She makes fun of everyone who she doesn't call her friends; she makes mean faces at people and throws stuff at me and some other girls in class even. I don't know why the teacher never seems to get after her about her behavior, it doesn't seem fair. I hope she stays away from this year, she is just terrible.

I really love catholic school, we get our bible teachings and we go to church during the week. I love learning about God and Jesus, it is comforting to know that God is always there for me. Will started first grade here with me this year at school. I just know he is going to love Miss Jasper, she is the best teacher ever she smells like a flower garden and her room is always bright and cheery, plus she has a smile that reminds me of an angel. She really helps her students learn everything clearly and she has the best reading books. When the bell rings we all line up by classroom which isn't hard; there is only one class and teacher per grade. Once everyone is lined up quietly, we say our morning prayers. What a great way to start every day praying and thanking God for another day. I am not too happy though to see my cousins have joined Will and I in attending school at St. Athanasius this year too. They are fun to play with sure but they are also full of trouble and lies. You know maybe it would do them some good to have some God and Jesus in their day, maybe then they wouldn't be so bad and annoying.

I don't know how many times I have been reminded about bringing my umbrella home from school. This is now the third umbrella that I have lost and my dad is really mad. He took me to Target to get a new one; he also told me I had better not let anything happen to this one or my ass is grass. So of course, like the wicked Cruella, my cousin Maryann yanked on a fly away string and burst the seam in my new 101 Dalmatians umbrella. She started laughing and all I could see was red, I was going to be in serious trouble and I knew it. So, I cornered her in the girl's bathroom and was strangling her with my umbrella. I figured if I was going to get into trouble because of her, I wasn't going down without really letting her have it too. Suddenly she doesn't think she is so funny, and the nuns that were pulling me off of her really didn't find anything funny with the whole situation. I was shouting at her to go to hell since she was as evil as Lucifer. Sister Tina told me to mind my mouth and told me I was in big trouble, she also said I should be ashamed of myself because God probably wasn't too happy with my behavior. I just rolled my eyes and thought what does she know? God wasn't going to save me from a butt spanking so why should he be upset that I defended myself in any way I thought right. The nuns took me straight to the principal who was herself a nun. I wasn't sorry which just made them all the more upset with me, and they really piled on the Hail Mary's and Our Father's; they said I needed to say as penance for my behavior and wrongs. My actions must have been really bad since I had so many hours of praying for my forgiveness; and how was praying in church going to get me forgiven? And shouldn't Maryann be at church praying to get forgiven for her wrongs? I don't fully understand why my pigheaded cousins never get what they deserve. I mean Maryann was in my class, but she was a whole year older than me, she knew better right? Maybe not she did get held back a year because she was struggling so much, so maybe she is still learning, maybe that is why she was struggling so hard with her behavior. Maryann gets all the perks, she even gets to go to the reading bus with the reading teacher. They keep telling me it is because she needs extra help, but I just don't see why she gets to read every day for an hour, she can just read whatever she wants and I can't. Was I not special? I thought I was because I am a princess after all. Or maybe I am not as important as I have thought all this time after all, because how could anyone tell me, a princess what I could and couldn't do?

I don't know what has gotten into me this year; I just can't seem to focus on my work. Not that I really care about doing my homework. I would rather watch tv, roller-skate, listen to music, read or just about anything else to avoid homework, it is just so boring and I just spent all day at school doing work. The school is so stupid and so is my teacher, after I spent all day working in the classroom, she has to send me home with work to complete from every subject. Oh, and my teacher is really mean she gave me a low mark on my short story, we had to write about someone who makes us happy and why. So, I wrote about my little brother Will, she said that I didn't put any real effort into my work and just slacked off taking the easy way out. That really made me not want to write again. I worked really hard on it and the teacher just didn't seem to like it. She said I could do better, but what does she know? I do love my brother and he does make me happy and a story about how he cheers me up seemed to be perfect. I think she should have to write a story; I bet she wouldn't be able to do any better. She passes these story assignments out every holiday, but I have never seen her write anything more than the math problems she is teaching us, on the board. I miss my old teachers they were nice, Mrs. Reed is totally mean. At least the school year is almost over; I am just not going to miss her, I can't wait to never see her mean face again. I am going to miss Frank though, and his cousin they are really cool to play four corners with, and do trick competitions on the bars. Just a few more weeks and Mrs. Reed will be out of my hair for good.

Well I did it again, I got myself in hot water and this time my mom and dad are super mad. I was up all night working on a story that was due today. Mom helped me write it, even after I told her I didn't want to do it. It was a great story about a magical leprechaun and all the tricks and mischief he gets into before being caught. I don't know why but when I got to school... I ...threw it right into the trash can. Maybe it's just the left over anger from the low score I got on my last paper. But with only a week left of school I was forced to have to retrieve it from the paper bin and hand it in anyway. I am not allowed to play outside for a week which means no fishing outside with Will. It is so unfair; I did say I didn't want to do it. But what do I know I am only eight; as the grownups keep reminding me?

Summer break has been really fun; Will and I have spent most of our summer surfing at the beach with mom. To fill the gaps in the time between the beach and the next trip to the beach we skate, ride bikes or fish. We have this big pool of water in the front yard, dad packs us lunch in the morning and then we collect our fishing poles to fish. We made the fishing poles ourselves with some sticks and some string. We collected worms from the garden for bait and would sit there all day sometimes to catch fish. We never did catch anything and it wasn't until the end of summer that I realized it wasn't a fishing hole but actually just a broken sprinkler. I don't think Will has figured that out yet, but dad will leave it be as long as it makes us happy and keeps us busy.

CHAPTER 5

ILLNESS

Fourth grade has been pretty cool. I am back at the same school I had attended in kindergarten; Los Cerritos Elementary. All my friends I remember from kindergarten are here and there are also a lot of new faces as well. This school is different from catholic school because it has two teachers and two class rooms for each grade, it's funny how I didn't know that when I was in kindergarten. I like the familiar smell of paper, paste, crayons and paint that fill the halls and the classrooms at this school. I love playing on the handball courts or doing tricks on the bars, even jump rope is fun. I do miss my friends back at St Athanasius, but Will and I had to stop attending because dad was laid off. Now he is working construction like he used to before. We don't have to wear uniforms any more either which is kind of cool.

The fourth grade is really fun, I really like science.

We do all kinds of science experiments like making volcanoes and learning about the weather. It really is some pretty interesting stuff. I love the reading club here at school and because I joined without my teacher asking me too, she buys me a new book from the scholastic flyers every time we get a new one. She is really proud of me for being so excited about reading, but the truth is I just love the feeling of getting lost in a good book and letting my imagination paint the picture for me. With a book I can imagine I am the character saving a pig, fighting dragons, or battling my terrible little brother; I could be anyone I wanted to be with a book and it was fun. I also join the school chorus group which is fun, we get to put on holiday and celebration shows for the parents and students. All my friends were also excited when we each got to write a letter to different companies asking them to donate for kids in need. We got so many awesome donations from all kinds of great places, like Lisa Frank, Scholastic, Mattel, and Hasbro just to name a few. We packed boxes for girls and for boys, and then the military men came and got them to deliver them to the kids overseas who had nothing. It felt really good to do something nice for people who needed to be shown some kindness, it made me really happy. Plus, we also learned that when we need to, people can really come together and give what they can to help others. I hope that I can do that again sometime.

I can't believe how fast the year is flying by it is already spring and my birthday is right around the corner. When we were flying kites at the park with mom and dad a few days ago I got bit by some strange bug. I didn't see what it was; I just felt it and swatted it away because it hurt so badly. A few hours after the bite my knee got hot and swollen but it wasn't hurting thank goodness. The next day I got up to ride bikes to the park with Will and although I rode my bike to the park, I couldn't ride it home so Will got off his bike too and we walked our bikes home. My leg was really hurting and my knee was starting to get a bit purplish in color and I felt very hot; by the time we made it home I was drenched in sweat.

Now sitting in Pizza Hut as we usually do on Friday family nights, I don't have an appetite and my arms have started hurting too; they are hurting so bad I can't even bring myself to go to the arcade area and play the games with Will. I can see the worry on mom's face and I feel terrible that I don't feel so good and that I am hurting so bad. I feel like I am really ruining our family fun night, but I have to ask mom to take me home because I can't cool down and I feel like I am going to throw up. When we got home, mom gave me some ibuprofen, so I hope after some sleep I will feel better.

Last night I was in so much pain I went straight to bed after we got home from Pizza Hut, I even skipped the movie. Today I woke up so sick, I am literally barfing all over the place and I can't keep anything down. My stomach feels like it is rolling all over and my legs and arms are killing me. I feel like there is fire burning my skin and there is sweat everywhere. Mom keeps telling me to drink and eat but I simply can't, I feel too dizzy and tired. I threw up on the floor running to the bathroom today and dad was so upset. He made me clean it up even though my arms are aching terribly bad. I have a doctor's appointment later so I have to get cleaned up, I hope that I can stand in the shower. I ended up taking a bath after all since standing in a wet shower didn't feel like a safe idea, I feel so weak.

After I got ready, mom picked me up and drove me to the doctor. I really didn't like him; I had to have an exam to check that nothing was wrong inside. I was upset that I had to take all my clothes off and be in a gown, even more upsetting was that he had to do and vaginal exam. I was so afraid and had never felt more naked than I did in that gown. I couldn't stop getting wave after wave of chills either. As my teeth chattered together while I waited for the doctor to come back into the room I thought, "I guess you can't be too careful." but I felt so sick and then adding to it a feeling of pure violation. I didn't understand what was going on or why I even felt that way. Mom apologized so many times. She even held my hand the whole time but it didn't make it any less traumatizing. When he put his finger in my privates and started pushing on my stomach I wanted to jump up and run away, I felt truly embarrassed. I was almost nine and didn't understand why nobody was talking to me they were all just talking to each other. I am not dumb, I can understand, and this was happening to me not them. I was so glad to be done with the doctor's appointment I couldn't get home fast enough.

It's been two weeks and I am still very sick. I can't walk or stand very well and I am always in pain. The many medications aren't helping, which is upsetting because I have to take them in suppository form since I can't keep anything down, yep that means mom has to help me and put it in my butt. That is so embarrassing and it is really uncomfortable, so I try to think about being well or pretty much anything else. So, since the medications don't seem to be helping me get better, it's back to the doctor for me. When the doctor is looking me over and taking my temperature, I can see that something is very wrong. Mom is crying and the doctor is talking about going next door; what is next door?

The Hospital is next door and when we walk over with my doctor in tow I am immediately put in a room, where I have to take everything off except my undies and put a gown on. It's cold and it smells like heavy duty cleaner, bleach and sick people; I am so scared. In fact, this seems to me to be the coldest spring ever, since I noticed that I can't seem to stop my teeth from chattering. Only I am being admitted to the hospital because my fever is so high it could mean I lose my eye sight, hearing or worse my brain function or life. The nurses and the doctor tell me I have to stop from getting chilled and keep a sheet on because it spikes your temperature when you get the chills. Mom finally told me what was going on, and I understood but was also suddenly wishing my little brother was with me. He always cheers me up, no matter how sick I feel or how much pain I am in; Will always makes everything seem so much better, he is such a silly little goof ball.

As soon as I climb into the big hospital bed the nurse comes in and hooks a bag on a metal stand that looks like a coat rack with wheels. Then she tells me she needs to start an IV and take some blood. I was used to blood being taken after all the doctor visits I had, but what was an IV? I quickly find out when she finds a vein on my outer arm and attaches some tubes that led from the bag of fluid to my arm. I hate being sick and I really hate how bad the hospital smells. The longer I am here the more I notice the hospital smells to me like sickness and death mixed in with fear. I can see other sick kids wheeling around in wheel chairs and wonder what it was we all did that was so bad for God to make us this sick. I was doing a lot of that lately; blaming God for my misfortunes. Actually, I think I have made a habit out of doing that because it is what mom and dad do too. It may sound unfair but I thought he would always be there, always look out for me, keep me safe, and now I am sick and afraid I might never get better. I know everyone would feel the same way I do if they were in my shoes, asking God why and blaming him for falling ill, everyone does it.

CHAPTER 6

RECOVERY

Today my fever spiked really high; at 106.7 and with the medications not breaking my fever they had no choice but too but to give me an ice bath. When they helped me out my gown and panties two nurses lifted me into the ice bath. One got my feet and the other held me up under my arms and they gently and slowly lowered me into the water. The water was so cold on my hot skin it felt like a million tiny needles were pricking me all over all at once, and I wanted to cry but I knew that wouldn't help or make things any more comfortable for me. They needed to get my fever down as fast as possible to save not only my hearing and sight but also my life. As I sit in the tub of ice water knowing that my life hangs in the balance, I pray to God to save me, I promise that I will be good from now on just so long as I get better. Can God even hear me, and if he can....is he even listening?

Isn't it funny how when you are sick suddenly everybody wants to see you and everybody is so nice? Even my wicked cousin Maryann is being nice to me. She had my uncle bring her by so she could leave me a stack of the hottest magazines. She wanted to be sure I would have something to read and also keep up with all the trendy actors and boy bands we loved so much. She brought them all Tiger Beat, Bop, Teen Beat, 16, 'Teen, BB, Teen People, YM, Jump, J-14, and BB, it was really thoughtful. I was thankful for the magazines because they gave me a distraction while the tv was playing the same movie the kids were watching in the kids' room, which was Willy Wonka and The Chocolate Factory. I really don't like that movie anymore, the first few times were ok but now I don't ever want to see it again. If I hear that oompa loompa song one more time I just might scream. Maryann was extra nice to me and helped me keep my hair back when I was throwing up and also complimented me on my new night gown my mom bought me. It made me miss playing with her and all my cousins. I promised her that if I got better, she could come stay over and we could ride bikes and skate all over. It would lots of fun and I sure did miss being able to use my legs and arms, and just feel free running and jumping.

So, I got a new nurse today his name is Allen and he is cute, I don't know why but every time he comes to check on me or give me meds, I feel fluttering in my tummy. Maybe that is just me feelings sick though. I can't explain the new feeling but I think I might have my first crush; lots of my friends have them on boys in our school. Oh, how I miss my friends; I have been in the hospital for two months and they still don't know what is wrong. I have lost so much weight I am now very underweight and weak. I have had the Priest come in and give me my last rights and blessings. This afternoon I got the results back from my bone scan and my bone marrow test, both normal. They put me on Naprosyn this morning to help manage the pain, and I broke out with a rash all over my body and in my mouth that felt like the worst sunburn ever. So now I am on a different pain medication and it seems to be helping. My fever finally broke today which means no more ice baths which I am thankful for, I don't think I could take another ice bath, they were terrible.

Tonight, Will is sleeping over with me in my hospital bed, and I am so thankful because I have missed him so much. I haven't seen him much since being in the hospital. I even spent my birthday and his in this miserable hospital. He came a few times with dad and ate the hospital dinners that I couldn't even look at without being sick. Will really loves the hospital food and can't seem to get enough of it. Allen left Winnie the Pooh hospital pajamas for Will to wear tonight. When he got here Will gave me a big hug and cuddled up right next to me in my bed and we watched Transformers and My Little Pony while we waited for the showing of The Wizard of Oz to start. We really loved The Wizard of Oz, the dream land that Dorothy goes to really feels like a great way to run away with her dog. I had fallen asleep cuddled up next to Will before the movie had even ended.

This morning I feel so hungry and nothing hurts. The doctors and nurses are all talking to mom and dad right now, mom seems upset yet relived at the same time. They never did figure out why I was so sick and in so much pain. And today I feel fine, they are going to release me in three days just so long as I remain well, but I will have to continue some of the medication for a week or so just for good measure. I am glad I will be going back to school soon I really missed my friends and my teacher, not to mention being outside in the sun. My teacher had me doing work from my hospital bed and reading, it was nice to have something to do in the hospital. My entire class wrote me letters to help me feel better too, and the teacher put them into a note book for me. It was so nice, and now to make up for lost class time I have to write all about what happened to me and how I felt, this way the class could hear about my experience with being so sick. I still feel funny not knowing what was happening to me exactly or why I was so sick?

My cat Rollie must have really missed me because when I got home, he ran to me and was rubbing his head into mine. I sure did miss him. He has been with me since we found him that first day of Kindergarten. He is all white and has blue eyes, and his fur is so soft. I love that he sleeps with me every night and keeps me warm and gives me companionship with unconditional love. We have always had so much fun together, I used to dress him up in baby clothes and push him around in a stroller with a bottle. He was such a silly cat. Now we cuddle and he sits with my while I do school work or read. I really like to pass my time reading these days. I enjoy going to the bookstore every other Friday, mom never says no to a book. When I get home from choosing my books, I curl up with Rollie and read out loud to him, he really likes story time.

I am so happy I feel better and can get back to life and fun. I still feel a little weak but I can't lay or sit down any longer, the doctors say I should take it easy but I just can't help it. I want to skate, ride bikes, or surf and feel the sun on my skin. Things might be looking up for me now.

CHAPTER 7

BAD INFLUENCE

Fifth grade just might be my year, there have been some new students that have moved into the neighborhood. They had to transfer into our school for their last year in elementary. There is one girl that I really like to hang around with that is new at school this year. Her name is Melissa and she is blonde like me and also has blue eyes like me. We seem to have so much in common we like the same boys, music, movies and activities. We have become really close but my two other best friends don't seem to like her much. Shannon and Chris just really need to give Melissa a chance, I know they will love her as much as I do. The only problem is Shannon's mom can be really strict, she doesn't even like to allow her any other friends over except me and Chris. I am sure that we can just hang out at my house or Melissa's house if that is what this is all about. It could also be that they are just jealous. They were giving me the cold shoulder for a while because I have been wearing bras for some time now and they just started to; I can't help it if I got boobs early. Not to mention I really don't like the attention all the boys give me all of the sudden either. Plus, Shannon and Chris were pretty upset the see that Melissa and I have the same hair and eye color, they think I only like her because she looks like me a little, and that is not it at all. I don't even want to know how upset they would be if they found out that Melissa and started our periods hours apart. It wasn't anything to brag about either, we spent that Saturday curled up watching movies. Those cramps are not a joke, I really wish I was lucky enough to have put that off for a couple more years.

I am so excited that the girls are all getting along now, we are going for a sleep over at Melissa house. We have the whole thing planned, Melissa is providing the refreshments, I am bringing the music, Shannon is bringing the movies and Chris is bringing the magazines. It is going to be so much fun because her mom is going to stay in her room and just let us have our girl talk and have fun. So yes, even though there will be an adult there it will be like we are totally alone.

Things could not have haven gotten any crazier than they did earlier tonight. Melissa had been having her older sister get alcohol for her for the past month, that she had been hiding in her closet for tonight. Everything was going really well and we all had our mixed drinks that we were sipping on and our popcorn watching movies and gossiping about the cutest boys. We all thought it was funny how last year none of them were cute or we just all seemed to grow up so fast all of the sudden, and we were all laughing. Suddenly Shannon thought we should call Steven her biggest crush, so we all giggled and called him.

Steven thought it was great getting a call from a group of girls, and decided to bring a bunch of guys over to crash our sleep over. Well, to say that didn't go over well is an understatement; Melissa's mom was really pissed. She yelled at all of us and sent the boys home after calling all of their moms, then she threatened to call our moms. Just when we went back to having fun and talking Chris started looking really sick. She drank too much and I swear she looked like her face changed to a shade of green I have only seen in the cartoons. I helped her get to her feet and walked her to the bathroom, she really reeked of alcohol and I was worried we would get caught. I held her hair back for her while she got sick over and over in the toilet, it made me flash back to last year when I was so sick and I felt bad for her. I rubbed her back the way mom did for me when I was sick and told her to just let it out, then I called for Melissa to see if she had any Gatorade or saltines to help her stomach settle. I remember mom made me drink Gatorade to hydrate and eat saltines to help my stomach feel better, plus I knew all too well that having anything in your stomach to throw up was better than bile.

The next morning when we all got up, we all had the worst headaches you can imagine. If this is what drinking makes you feel like I wonder why adults do it all the time. I felt like my eyes were going to pop out of my head, but I always carry ibuprofen on me now just in case I really start to feel pain, so I will just take some of that now. Mom told me that I should only take two tablets and no more than that, plus she writes it on the bottle. I can't give any to the other girls because mom told me I am not allowed to even tell anyone I have it and never allowed to give it to anyone else. I really hope that the girls feel better later so we can still go roller blading, I just got a new pair of blades I want to break in.

Well, what can I say? Some people just don't know how to hideout or keep their mouth shut. Shannon told her mom she had a really bad headache and because she didn't have a fever, she was going to take her to urgent care. Yeah Shannon's mom is one of those moms who worries about every little bump and scrape. So, Shannon freaked out and spilled the beans on all of us. She told her mom everything. She even told her about the boys coming over, which makes no sense to me because Melissa's mom wasn't going to nark after she laid into us already. I am so mad at Shannon because now we are all grounded and I will be lucky to even be allowed to still hangout with Melissa. I mean of all the moms that could have found out and called my parents it had to be Shannon's mom? That bitch is straight up on another level or being a world class worry wart and exaggerating the truth. I guess her mother never warned her about how much exaggerating can get you in hot water unless you are an actor. Melissa is really mad at Shannon to, she could have just gone to the urgent care or told on herself why all of us? I could kind of see Melissa's point even if I did think it was a little harsh. I mean has she even met Shannon mom? I am pretty sure even her own husband is afraid of her the way he seems to always be rushing out, or needed to go to bed right after work and dinner. I don't think I have ever really seen them talking. Of course, I would have to ask Shannon about my hunches because I don't want to be an exaggerator.

Over the past few months the girls and I have only hung out in a group at school, the other girls still are not allowed to hang out with Melissa. Outside of school I am being allowed to hang around with Melissa so long as my mom makes it clear each time that her mom has to be in the room with us, or if we are in Melissa's room the door has to be open. I guess it is a pretty good rule considering the trouble we got into at the sleep over. I try to split my time between Melissa, Shannon and Chris on the weekends, because it just seems fair to everyone that way. Shannon and Chris told me that they don't really care to hang out with Melissa anymore and I guess I am starting to see why. All Melissa wants to talk about is boys, which wouldn't be a problem because let's face it we all do ever since the beginning of the year when we noticed we might actually like them now, and that maybe they don't have cooties. It is just the way she talks is so grown up, she talks about kissing and touching and even sex. I don't think she has actually done any of those things but I am not completely sure. The only things I know for sure is that her mom is raising her and her sister alone and has to be on medicine to help her not cry so much, and her dad is in prison and she is not allowed to write him or talk to him. Her sister usually seems pissed off at everything but so do her friends, her mom said that is just how teenagers act. I guess with all the mixed-up things in her life she just wants to seem cool so Melissa takes the boy talk to an extreme. I have also noticed that when she stays at my house some of my things go missing. Chris had mentioned that her portable cd player went missing from her backpack last week when Melissa was watching her bag at lunch while she went to buy milk. I never even thought that Melissa might have taken it until recently.

I am waiting outside the movie theater for Melissa

to get here, I rode my bike over and can't wait until she gets here because I am really thirsty and want to get a soda pop.

I can't believe that Melissa brought some guy with her. They came walking up together holding hands and she had the cheesiest smile on her face, which for her was silly. She never really smiles because she hates that she has braces, and all we hear are complaints about how much they cut up her lips when she smiles. When we were getting closer to the ticket window Melissa says we are changing our plans and seeing Fair Game instead of Man of the House. I protested and said, "but it is a R rated movie and we can't even get in to see it, and why would we want to watch that movie anyway?" The third wheel she brought along snapped back at me, "because Cindy Crawford is in it and she is sexy as fuck; you girls should all want to be sexy like her." I just stood there and didn't say a word, I was really angry but since he said he would be paying, I didn't protest further, I already looked like a fool.

In the line to get snacks and drinks Melissa told me that he was in college and she seemed really excited about it. I really couldn't understand why she thought that was so great he seemed to me, really too old for me to even want to talk to him; or maybe it was just something else I am sensing that is putting me off about him. I rolled my eyes grabbed my drink and popcorn and we headed in to grab our seats. As I walked in planning to head to the middle row and sit half way down like we always did Melissa grabs my arm and says she is sitting in the back with Matthew. Oh it has a name, this strange guy that was rude enough to not introduce himself to me at all and she is smitten over. I told her I wanted her to sit with me in our regular seats but she said, "I am going to sit in the back row with Matt, he likes blowjobs while he watches Cindy. You should come and sit with us I think he wants you to give him one too." I really thought I was going to throw up or at least run away, the thought of what she was saying was disgusting. Instead I just said, "No you go ahead with that, I am just going to go ahead and sit where we usually do."

Through the entire movie all I could do was cry, I couldn't stop thinking about what Melissa said and what she was doing back there. I was sickened by the thought of it and felt I wasn't such a great friend because I didn't feel right about keeping this secret. Should I keep this a secret? I wanted tell on her, this didn't feel right. I mean yeah, she always talks about boys and doing all these nasty things with them but I never thought she was or would actually do them, and certainly not with a grown up. I didn't know what I could say to make her stop but it was worth a try to say something. Maybe I could get her to listen to me because something about all of this just feels wrong to me, in my heart and in my gut, it just doesn't feel good.

I invited Melissa over to my house to hangout, I really needed to talk to her. When she got to my house we went to my room and I tried to act like everything was fine because I didn't know how she was going to react. She starting talking about Matt and how they went back to his place after the movie and had sex. She told me that he loved her and that when she turns sixteen, they are going to Kansas to get married. That is when I felt the word vomit just spilling out of my mouth. I told her that Matt seemed creepy to me and that it didn't feel right to me that she is giving him blowjobs and sex. I pleaded with her to stop and to just go back to how things were before just hanging out and having fun. Going to the movies and watching the movies we normally would. She got really upset and started crying and told me I was acting like such a child. I had to leave the room to collect myself in the bathroom I didn't want her to see me cry or let her know that she really hurt my feelings. I just thought about how excited we were to go to camp with our class before the end of the year in two weeks. We even asked the teacher to put us in the same cabin, but I wasn't sure that I could face her and act like what she was doing was ok.

When I came out of the bathroom Melissa was gone. My drawers were open and she left a note. "Sorry I took your favorite bra but since we are the only two girls in our class wearing the same size, I needed it. If you want to stay a baby that is fine but I plan to make these B cups look sexy for Matt. You should really just get over yourself and have sex already because that is what boys want, it's what they like and you will to. Bye dork!"

When I read that note I felt the heat of anger wash over, me and I three way called Shannon and Chris to tell them I agreed with them about keeping our distance from Melissa. I kept her secret and didn't mention Matt and the blowjobs, sex or the movie theater. I just wasn't a snitch like that and it was her life anyway. I just told them that I think she has been stealing from me and I wasn't sure what I thought about how she talks about boys. Chris told me she thought she had stolen her portable cd player out her backpack and Shannon said she was all for talking about boys but the making out and sex talk really made her uncomfortable. I didn't realize that they had felt so strongly about this for so long because I guess we did drift a little when Melissa showed up. I wish that we were all going to be in a cabin together at camp now, but it is too late to make changes.

CHAPTER 8

LOSS OF INNOCENCE

The two fifth-grade classes are on the school buses now heading to Camp Hi-Hill and it is so exciting. This week is going to be so much fun and going to camp is like a rite of passage, like your golden ticket to visit Wonka's factory. It is the first huge step toward not be a little kid any more. Sure, the teachers of both the fifth-grade classes are coming along and the counselors at the camp are really just college students trying to get extracurricular credit for doing it, but other than that it will be something that has been just out of reach for our grubby digits, free of parents. Or at least that is what the teachers have said, they want us to learn survival skills, independence and some cool stuff about nature and the outdoors. I am glad that we can sit next to anyone we want on the bus ride over. Shannon, Chris and I all squeezed onto the same bus bench and we can't stop talking about what camp might be like. Melissa seems to have made a new friend she is sitting with Mark a few rows ahead of us. I try not to pay too much attention or let myself care that she is even on the bus at all; even though I could feel them looking back, and I even caught some of the looks and whispers.

When I got off the bus, I could smell the fresh air, everything smelled so crisp and there was a faint smell of plants and wild flowers in the air. Everything was so green and the sky was clear and a beautiful shade of blue, it was all so beautiful. The crunch of dirt and gravel on the paths was a welcomed new sensation in comparison to the city sidewalks of cement. The paths lead us to cabins and the mess hall where they held all meals. We all gathered at the mess hall first and got lunch while one of the teachers talked about the plan for the day and what was expected from us in terms of behavior at all times. Then one of the camp counselors took over and explained the dos and do NOTs of cabin and camp rules and what to do if we noticed any rules being broken and who to talk to about it. Then the counselor talked about how we have to stay in our own cabins, boys and girls may not be in a cabin together without a counselor or teacher supervising us, no holding hands unless we are helping a friend up, no wandering around alone or away from our group, we have to shower every night before bed, curfew is at 9:30 pm and lights out is 10 pm. If we see or hear anything or feel that any students or even the counselors are breaking any rules, we are to report it to the lead counselor Benny or to one of the teachers. Because two schools always did camp together, to encourage meeting new people and making new friends, the roar of laughter at the idea that any of us would nark, was louder than ever.

After lunch was over, we went to our cabins to find out who was in our cabin and get to know the each other. We also found out what cabin we would be doing excursions with in a group. On the way to the cabin I thought just for a second that I saw Matt headed to one of the cabins. I really tried to put it out of my head and even laughed a little inside because that couldn't have been possible. What are the odds that he would be here and we are here? Then I looked over at Melissa wondering if she was still "dating" him, I really hope not.

The first night at camp we sat under the stars to learn about the constellations. To my horror Matt was there, he is a counselor here for college credit on his university application. I hated that he was even talking to me and Melissa seems overly happy about it, so I am half certain that they are still an item, but I can't be one hundred percent sure. Matt kept rubbing my shoulders and when I asked him to stop, he said he was just trying to keep me warm. I had a sweatshirt on and I was pretty comfortable and all I wanted for him to do was stop fucking touching me! I hated him and blamed him for ruining my friendship with Melissa. We weren't mean to each other or anything like that; as far as I could tell anyway, we just don't talk or hangout. It is just a byproduct of having very different views on right and wrong. Plus, I am still really mad at her for stealing my bra, she wears it all the time, I think she is just trying to get to me but I just think it is gross. Who steals or wears someone else's under garments? It's pretty much a trashy thing to do if you ask me and I don't much care for it but I am not doing it so why should I care what she wears? Besides all that if she really needed a bra, I would have given it to her if she just would have asked me.

When we got back to our cabin and our counselor Jane told us that we could shower, but to go to bed by 10 pm… lights out. She said that the counselors have a bond fire every night and just hangout, that they would be checking on us through the night. Honestly, Jane made me feel safe about the night schedule and everything seemed fair to me about 10 pm lights out, it gave us some time to be ourselves away from adults and do our own thing so, I didn't mind.

When all the other girls in the cabin were showering, they were so LOUD… I decided to sit down and read the letter mom tucked into the new book that she bought me for the trip. I am glad that she also thought ahead and packed a book light too, because I really enjoy reading before bed. After reading mom's letter that talked about how she was going to miss me but she was hopeful I would have fun, I started my book. I did what I did at home in a loud house, I tuned the loud and rowdy girls out while I read silently, in a book time warp. At some point without noticing I must have turned the book light on; when I looked up from my book everyone was in bed sleeping so I checked the time, it was only 9:45 pm. I guess everyone was really tired from all the excitement of the first day here. So, I just gathered my toiletries bag and my towel and headed to the shower stall.

When I walk into the showers, I am painfully aware of how loud the door creaks. I switch the lights on and it dawns on me that I didn't notice that the toilet stalls and sinks were on the other side of the room. There are three stalls and three sinks on one side and six shower stalls on the other side. The room has white and light green tiles and smells like bleach and the wood of the cabin surrounding it. As I stand under the hot shower water and wash my legs, I get this sinking feeling that someone is watching me. When I turn around, I can see a shadow of a person on the other side of the shower curtain. It startled me a bit at first like a mouse caught in the clawed paws of a cat, but then I thought maybe one of the other girls might need something. I stood silent listening for just a few seconds.

"Who is there? Are you ok!" I call out.

"Oh, I am just fine darlin!" A voice I didn't want to hear answered me back.

It was Matt, why was he in the cabin? Why was he in the shower room and how long has he been standing there? Was he in the cabin before I got in the shower, and if so when did he come in? My mind is racing thinking of all these questions but my mouth won't let the words come out. Finally, after what seemed like minutes, I manage to ask him what he is doing in the cabin shower room. He tells me it was his turn to do the cabin checks to make sure everyone was in bed. Just then he pulls the shower curtain open and he is completely naked. I start to shake and my body suddenly feel numb from the fear of him being so close to me naked. He grabs me and shoves me against the shower wall and whispers to me that I am going to be a good girl and not scream. I can't help but stand frozen not allowing my mind to really absorb the words coming out of his mouth or his actions. It is as if I am floating away from body as he grabs my right breast with his hand and lowers his head and starts sucking on my nipple. With his other hand he starts rubbing me between the legs and I can feel tears start to run down my face. I close my eyes and pray for God to help me, to whisk me away from the moment and save me, but when I open my eyes, I am still here in this damn shower stall and he is still touching me. When Matt leans in to whisper in my ear again I can smell the pungent aroma of alcohol on his breath. He is keeps telling me I am sexy and all I want to do throw up or scream for help, but I am so afraid I can't do anything but stand there.

When Matt hears a whimper escape from me, he covers my mouth and tells me I have to stay quiet and do what he says or he will hurt me. Now it's official and I know I am real, serious danger with no way out. When he asks me if I understand what he has just said, I nod and he takes his hand away from my mouth and starts licking and suckling at my nipples. I have never felt more naked or more afraid in my entire life as I do now. He is putting his fingers in my vagina and tells me he is going to love making me cum like the sexy little bitch I am, and I just shake my head in a forced nod and try to fight back the tears. My mind won't stop screaming to me, "Why is this happening to me?"

Matt gets down on his knees and lifts my leg over his shoulder pushes my back harder against the shower wall and puts his mouth on my vagina and starts licking me. I have no idea what is happening to me or why my body is feeling so good when my mind and heart are feeling so bad and hurt. As my legs start to quiver and shake another whimper escapes me but this time Matt just smiles. And as he stands up quickly, I flinch thinking he is going to hurt me like he promised to do if I wasn't quiet, but he doesn't hit me. He lifts me up while wrapping my legs around him and tells me, "You are so fucking sexy and I have wanted you since the moment I saw you!" I have to look away so he can't see the tears that start to fall down my face. I mean was he crazy? I don't want this; did he even consider that? When he slides me down onto his penis it hurts and I try not to whimper or cry biting my lips closed with my teeth, out of fear. I can feel him filling up my vagina as he kisses my closed mouth and tells me, "You have a perfect little pussy and amazing tits. You are my little whore now, I am going to fill you up with my love potion." The words he said were so disgusting along the pain in between my legs and the smell of the alcohol on his breath; it was all making me really sick and I just want to wake up from the horrible nightmare.

When Matt was finished and was getting dried off and dressed, I was sitting on the shower floor with blood running down my leg. My vagina was throbbing in a mix of heat and pain and I was just crying praying that it would all stop. Before Matt left, he turned around and grabbed me by the throat and told me this was our little secret and if I even thought about telling anyone he would kill me and my whole family. That was it I could never tell another living soul I couldn't give this guy a reason to murder me and my family…..my little William.

After Matt left, I stood up and started scrubbing my skin until it hurt. It didn't seem to matter how much or how hard I scrubbed I still felt dirty. When the water got cold, I got out of the shower and put my pajamas on and I climbed into my bed. When I looked over at Melissa's bed, she sat up smiling and gave me a thumbs up. Did she know that Matt was here, she had to have known because why else was she awake? I can't believe she would set me up like that but I knew she had something to do with what just happened, or at least she knew. I still felt sick and my vagina was still throbbing so it was hard to fall asleep. I looked at the clock and it was 11:34 pm so I rolled over and pulled the blanket over my face, angry…hurt…. afraid and cried myself to sleep.

The sun came up in the morning the alarm in the cabin woke us all up at 7:30 am. Jane was getting up with us and I wondered when had she gotten back to the cabin, and why wasn't she back sooner last night if she was going to sleep in her bed in the cabin anyway? I was mad at her for leaving us alone because maybe if she was here all night, Matt couldn't have forced me to have sex with him. I had to push the thoughts aside for now and get ready to go eat breakfast, even though I wasn't hungry because I still felt a little sick. On our walk over to the mess hall for breakfast, Melissa caught up to me and starting walking with me. She asked me," so how does it feel to be a woman now? Don't you feel better not being a part of the dork squad?" I felt like my heart was shattering into a million tiny pieces right now and I fought back the tears that were threatening to flood out of my eyes like waterfall.

"You know what he did to me and you think that it is ok? What is wrong with you Melissa!"

"Of course, I know silly. I helped him figure out

how he could get you to just have sex with him already, last night while we were studying the constellations. I mean it wasn't exactly a secret that he wants you, I told you that at the theater remember?"

"What is your problem? And what do you mean he wants me? That is never going to happen again, I can't do that again I will die."

"Well I guess you are going to die then! You are so lame, you're such a little cry baby. I should have known you would act like this and make a big deal out it. You are so stupid, I told you that is what girls are supposed to do with boys."

"Number one I can't believe you would do this to me, and number two it doesn't feel right and you both make me sick."

As I walked away from Melissa, I let the tears rush down my face. I could feel the wetness on my face and taste the salt in my tears and it made me think about the threat that Matt had made. I thought that maybe I could find a way to tell someone, but then I thought about the fact that Melissa knows where I live. I am sure that bitch would tell Matt and he would make good on his promise to hurt my family; I need to protect my little brother Will from his evil clutches. I had better wipe my face and act normal before someone see me like this.

CHAPTER 9

VICTIM MENTALITY

I am still in shock that Melissa had a hand in what happen last night. We used to be such great friends and I never thought she would do anything to hurt me, now it is clear she is not the person I thought she was. She is just an evil wicked person and I hate her for being a part of Matt taking sex from me. I will just keep my head down and focus on the excursions and sticking with the group from here on out.

Tonight, we are testing our skills of using the stars to find our way on the trails. Three cabins are in our group and there is one counselor with the group telling us when we can start our walk on the trails to find our way to our goal point. There are two more counselors along the trail "hiding" to make sure nobody gets lost and one with a flash light to wait for us at the finish line. This should be fun! A few students go before me, we have to wait three whole minutes in between the each person starting on the walk. When is it my turn to start walking I am excited to do this but also scared I might get lost, I can hear and feel the dirty and gravel under my feet and the night air is cool and damp as I take in a huge gulp.

Half way into the walk I hear something that sounds like foot steps behind me, my stomach jumps into my throat and I stop walking. I really hope that I am not being tracked by some wild animal. Just as the though passes through my mind I feel a hand on my arm, I turn to see that it is Matt.

"What do you want?"

"I want you, sexy!"

"I don't want to have sex with you and I don't want you touching me either."

Matt got really angry after I got those words out of my mouth, he grabbed me by the throat and said, "don't forget that I will kill you and your family if you don't do what I say and keep your mouth shut, you little bitch."

So, I nodded my head and followed him off the trail into the dense bushes. I knew that he wasn't worried about getting caught because he didn't look or act like he was at all. Once we reached a wide-open area in the bushes and trees, he grabbed me around the waist and pulled me to him. I could smell the soap he used and feel the heat of his body on mine and it made me sick. He put his hand in my pants and worked his fingers in between my vagina lips and started rubbing, I couldn't help the shakes and quakes through my legs and it made me feel ashamed and broken. He made me get on my knees then he pulled his pants down and put his penis in my mouth. I started to cry as he told me, "knock it off and move your head back and forth keeping your tongue on my cock." He was making me give him a blowjob and I could smell the aroma of his privates and tasted the salt of the flesh. I wanted to throw up and he kept jamming his penis into my throat making that urge even stronger. Then he told me to pull my pants and panties down and get on my hands and knees I started shaking but did what he said. He got behind me and got on his knees but he had to lift me off my knees, then and he rammed his penis inside me hard, it hurt so bad I almost screamed but I bit my lip to keep from making noise. As he was pumping himself in and out of me, I continued to bite my lip until I broke the skin tasting my own blood. I let the blood run down my lip and watched it drip in the dirt as I let my mind drift away from me; I just disconnected from the horror and pain. When he was about to give me his "love juice" as he called it, he started ramming into me harder and rougher and the pain was almost more than I could bare. I couldn't help but whimper and cry. He said, "oh fuck yeah baby I am gonna cum and fill that tight little pussy up." He let out a loud moan and I could feel his body jerk and the pulsing of his penis that was deep inside of me, I just hung my head and cried. When he pulled himself out of me some of his cum started to drip down toward the front of my vagina so he bent down and licked me spreading my lips enough to circle his tongue and flick it until I felt a wave of extreme pleasure my body melted in release all while shaking. Then he licked me from the front of my vagina all the up to my butt hole. How disgusting! Then he got up and pulled his pants on and told me to do the same. I tried to keep my head down so he couldn't see my face, and I didn't want to see. When he noticed I was crying he said, "give me a break you little slut, you know you love it. In fact, you love it so much I am going to fuck that tight little cunt of yours as much as I can."

"Please just leave me alone now you got what you wanted and it hurts me, I don't like it." I protested.

"You better get used to it, and don't worry it will stop hurting you will love it so just shut up because you know you want me. I know you love fucking me and keeping me happy right, or else. Oh, and don't forget to keep your mouth shut."

I suddenly felt a wake of nausea I couldn't choke back and I threw up in the bushes until my body felt empty and numb. Then he grabbed me by the arm and marched me back to the trail. When we got back onto the trail there was a counselor there walking the trail to ensure everyone had made it safely to the destination point before the last three kids could walk it. Matt looked unfazed by this and simply said, "This one seems to have almost gotten herself lost. She seems a bit scared but I found her. Told her she needs to pay attention to where she is going and not just look up at the stars the whole time she is walking, silly kid." The other counselor didn't even question his story he just shook his finger in my face and said I had ought to be more careful. The other counselor motioned for me to go ahead and join the group while he and Matt stayed behind to talk. I couldn't help but wonder if he knew what really happened, and if he did maybe everyone knew about Matt. There was no help for me here, even if I felt safe enough to tell someone.

My group got back to our cabin at 9:15 pm and we were so ready for bed we all couldn't wait to take showers. This time I rushed into the shower stall; I couldn't be alone in the showers ever again and I knew that. Once we were dressed and ready for bed Jane said good night then headed out to hang out with the other counselors.

I don't know when I fell asleep or what time it is now, all I know is I woke up to hand over my mouth. It's Matt again and he is telling me to be quiet and follow him. He is taking me to a small cabin like building that I think is used to hold nature books, the library! I love books so much I remembered someone had mentioned it earlier. When we get inside, he locks the door and turns to me pulling me to him, one quick glance around and I see that this is not the library at all. He lifts me up and tells me to kiss him, I comply and follow all his instructions and his lead because I know the stakes all too well now. He sets me down and takes my night shirt off exposing my breasts, and he leans down and starts kissing them and licking my nipples. I try to cover my nipples out of shame of them reacting to his lapping and kissing, but he pushes my arms away. Then he tells me to lay down and he takes his clothes off while I stare at the ceiling trying to convince myself that this is just a bad dream. My vagina is still sore and I am scared and worried about the pain to come.

Matt kneels down and crawls on top of me and I

can feel the heat and the weight of his body, I can also and smell the alcohol he has been drinking. He is kissing my neck and kneading at my breast with one hand and rolling my nipple and holding himself up with the other hand. Then he moves down spreading my legs open and bending my knees, then he starts licking me and the same shameful wash of pleasure takes me and I start to cry. Then he leans back slightly and rubs his hard penis along the outside of my vagina and then slips it in and the pain is like fire because I am swollen and raw. Then he puts his arm under me and rolls us so that I am on top of him and he tells me to rock my hips. I do it because I know his threats are real. As I am rocking and moving, I can feel him going in and out of me slightly and he has his hand rubbing my vagina. He asks me if I like the way he rubs my clit and I nod yes so, he doesn't get mad. Then suddenly I can feel my body get tight and it starts to shake in wave after wave of pleasure. And it can't help but whimper and cry because I am so ashamed. My mind knew that something about this was wrong and it did physically hurt but then on the other edge of this double-edged sword my body was also enjoying it physically too. It was the ultimate betrayal on myself, my body betrayed my mind, heart and soul. Matt then grabbed me by my butt and started lifting me and slamming down onto him and it made me whimper and cry in pain. He said he must have drank, too much so we had to try something else. He told me to get on my hands and knees and then I felt the most horrible pain as he shoved his penis into my butt. I could NOT control it I let out a scream. He then smacked my butt as hard as he could and told me to shut the fuck up. I was crying and whimpering in pain as he pumped himself in and out of my butt it hurt so bad, I couldn't wait for him to be done. He was getting rougher and rougher and then he pulled himself out of me and made me suck his penis until he came in my mouth.

When he took me back to my cabin, I went into the bathroom to clean myself up. I wasn't sure why I felt wet and decided to use some wipes that were in the cabin bathroom to clean up before I dried my private areas off. When I sat down on the toilet I looked down and noticed the blood in my panties and then I started wiping. The blood was coming from my butt, I knew it was sore but I didn't think it was bleeding. I put a panty liner on and went out to the sinks to wash my mouth out and brush my teeth. I could still taste the nasty flavor of Matts cum in my mouth and I wanted it gone.

When I got back in bed, I laid there for a minute thinking about what I could have done to deserve all this. I also pondered how far my vocabulary has stretched as well as my knowledge of the new-found words and their meanings; was this the foul language of cursed words I didn't fully comprehend until now? I guess I really was a woman now, like it or not.

Over the next two days Matt continued to corner me at every opportunity he could and wake me up in the night to make me have sex with him. Each time it felt like I was breaking a little more. I was raw and in pain, my body ached all over and I couldn't wait until I could leave for home. Matt even pointed me out and lied saying that he had seen me holding hands on a hike with one of the boys in our group. The other counselors and the teacher looked shocked at first, but then I got in trouble and had to sit out during art time when they were sanding their memory logs with none other than Matt. Of course, he used that time to force sex on me again. FUCK CAMP!

On Friday at noon I think I was the first one on the buses. I felt safe when Shannon and Chris came and squeezed in next to me. While Shannon and Chris talked about all the fun they had, I stayed quiet and looked out the window. I was just happy to be on my way home. I missed my loud family and the safety of a book in my own room. When the buses finally pulled up to the school at four pm, I was happy to see mom waiting for me. When I got off the bus, I ran to her and gave her the biggest longest hug and started to cry. I told her it was because I missed her so much which was only half the truth. I gave mom a soft smile and asked her to pick up some In-N-Out since it was my favorite burger joint.

While mom made the food run, I took the opportunity to take a shower. I turned the water on as hot as I could stand it and scrubbed my skin until it was red and nearly raw. Once I felt like I had scrubbed the vileness of camp away, I stepped out of the shower and got dressed. I could smell the amazing scent of freshly cooked burgers as soon as I opened the bathroom door and I couldn't wait to eat with my family.

CHAPTER 10

SELF PITY

The last two weeks of school and the first two weeks of summer have been a blur. I am in and out of deep thought so much these days I can't seem to keep track of my time.

After school ended and I had my fifth-grade promotion celebration at the park with both fifth grade classes; I just mostly stated in my room. I have been listening to a lot of music and just passing my time reading. Don't get me wrong I have gone to the beach with Will and mom every weekend and still do the family Fridays, I just slink away when I can and do my own thing. I haven't even really spoken to Shannon and Chris this summer and I hope they hav-e been having the best summer.

I just keeping think about everything that has happened to me in my life, all the bad things. I can't help but wonder what I did for God to punish me so much and never help me. Why when I prayed for God to save me or protect me, did he just leave me to danger and pain? Why is God so mad at me? You know if God would have helped me even just once I would have been able to forgive him, but this has gone too far. I really hate God for all he has done to me and let happen to me.

I mean Shannon always has all the coolest new stuff and she is always happy. Chris has parents that let her do almost anything she wants and they take her to some really cool places like DisneyWorld in Florida. Plus, they haven't gotten their periods yet which means no bleeding and cramping and freedom to swim whenever they please. Melissa is happy going along on her marry way in life. She gets whatever she wants; she is dating that guy Mark now and I am sure they are having sex. News travels fast when you brag as much as she does. I really wish I had a room as big as hers too, her mom gave her the master bedroom because she wanted it. She let her decorate it all herself too, my mom would have a cow and start yelling through the house if I asked her if I could decorate my room. She would complain about how long it takes dad to finish anything and then he would start yelling and it would turn into a circus.

My mind keeps haunting me with shame and embarrassment about the week at camp. I don't really know for sure what happened to me but it is like Matt took a piece of me. I don't feel whole anymore and my mind feels full of thoughts and questions of memories and confusion. I don't even like going to church anymore since that week, it feels like a lie. I wish I could tell mom or even

Shannon and Chris everything in my head but I can't. Matt was serious and he knows where I live too, because he kept one of the envelopes from one of the letters from mom and dad, when I was at camp.

I don't know why all this shit is happening to me. I must be really bad at life or I am doing something wrong, but I just need life to get better. Maybe if I focus on school and myself more things will go back to the way were and life will be easy. I need to find happiness in life because I hate feeling like this voided innocence that and I know it would break mom's heart if she thought I wasn't happy.

CHAPTER 11

NEW BEGINNINGS

I am so happy to be in middle school this year. I am leaving the darkness of last year behind me and burying all the nastiness and hurt along with it. I am not sure what to expect this year but it has to better than last year. After starting my period and the creep counselor at Camp Hi-Hill, I am ready to forget. I am going to put all those memories and pains in a black box inside my mind and lock them away deep inside my brain. This is a new school and a fresh start.

When I walk on campus and down the halls every morning, I can smell the faint smell of cleaner and the dingy smell of an old building. Navigating around school to different classes isn't as difficult as I thought it would be. This school is bigger than my elementary school and there are so many students here, even though there are only three grades, that there are two lunch periods. I have the early lunch period and sit with Shannon and Chris at lunch every day. We don't have any of the same classes together, although we do have some of the same teachers and classes at different periods in the day. It is kind of funny how that worked out. There is a mix of kids from the two elementary schools in the area that attend school here this year. Then the other two grades of kids just add to all the new faces I see every day. When I am not passing time reading, I am people watching, and I pretty much see everything. Besides knowing everything about the hottest new books, I also know what groups of people stand where and who the group consists of. I can tell you who the couples are and who the enemies are. It is really funny when you think about how the adults don't see how complex we really are and how much we really are like them. Maybe that is what it means when they say kids are a mirror of what they see and hear. We basically just mimic what we see and hear the adults doing.

Sixth grade is going to amazingly well here at Hughes middle school; the school I am attending which means almost all my friends from the fifth grade are attending here with me and it all makes everything easier and less stressful. We have to wear uniforms now that public schools have made uniforms mandatory. I don't mind, it is so much easier to get ready in the morning; not having to stress about what to wear, if it is in style or if the other kids will laugh at you. The only thing I hate about the uniforms is that they don't breathe that well so in the hot weather you are going to be uncomfortable, hot and sticky.

I love how we go to different classes with

different teachers every hour. It really is cool to not sit in the same room with the same teacher all day, especially if the teacher just has it out for you or is a complete jerk. Plus, I like to be able to get up and stretch my legs and hand off notes between Shannon, Chris and myself when we pass each other in the halls. It helps us to keep up on the school gossip and boy talk since we only really talk at lunch every day. Well they talk and I mostly listen. We don't start or spread the rumors we keep the ones we hear between us, we have just never been those type of girls and probably never will be. I would never want to hurt anyone else with my words or actions, hurting others does NOT make you cool in my book, it just makes you an asshole. That is why when I heard that there was a rumor going around about some mystery girl who was having sex at camp last year with one of the counselors, my heart stopped, or at least I thought it did. I knew exactly who started the rumor too, as soon as I heard it, I knew it had to have been Melissa. Now I have to corner that bitch and tell her to keep her trap shut because if Matt finds out, he will kill her or both of us, what a stupid disgusting trash panda. What does she get out of this anyway, to go out of her way to spread a rumor like that she would have to be getting something out of it; right?

In fourth period I cornered Melissa before the chorus teacher got in, and I told her to keep her big mouth shut. I told her I heard the rumor and knew it was her that started it, she tried to laugh it off. She sure did change her tune when I told her he threatened me which means her would hurt her to if he even thought she said something. For the first time since I met Melissa, I saw real fear in her eyes and she apologized and agreed to keep her silence on the subject. My last period of the day is physical education otherwise known as PE. I really didn't care for PE other than the fact that, in one of the other PE classes there is a boy that really catches my eye, he is so cute. He has brown hair, green eyes and is taller than me. When he walks past me in the halls, I can smell his cologne and the smell is so fresh and manly I can't help but breathe it in. I find that I can't stop staring at him and end up catching a ball in the face every now and then because of it. How embarrassing! All of this is very new and interesting because I still am not comfortable around boys one hundred percent but I still find some of them cute. I really hope I can get by all of these feelings that are confusing my mind.

So that cute boy is an eighth grader and his name is Ken. He is also in the boys chorus, I am in the junior chorus with all the other sixth graders and some seventh graders. I wish I was in the senior chorus because the boys always stand to applaud them. It makes me feel like such a little girl that the boys only seem to favor the senior girls chorus and sometimes it hurts the entire junior groups feelings. It is ok though because Ken found out how hurt it made our feelings so he got the rest of the boys chorus to join him in standing and applauding us at our last school concert. It was so nice and it made me feel so special.

CHAPTER 12

THE CHASE

Things have really turned upside down for me recently. After my eleventh birthday I just suddenly lost interest in school. Some of the class work was really easy and other stuff was really difficult for me. In English class we had two assignments I just bombed. The first one was a paper on our families and what makes them so special to us. The teacher said it would help us to write about positive things we hold dear and it would help us learn more about who we are. The problem is I don't remember why I love my family or what makes them so great. I love my family just because I do. But what is so great about them? I don't know, Will and I have been fighting so much lately, he has his friends and I have mine. Sure, we still hangout sometimes and roller blade or ride our bikes around the neighborhood and we did find a litter of wild kittens we found homes for together, but things are just not like old times. Sometimes I even feel like I miss Will even when we are sitting right next to each other. We don't share secrets anymore and maybe that is because I can't tell him my biggest secret; maybe it was my fault we were fighting so much. Then mom and dad have been yelling at me so much and yelling at each other. They complain to themselves but out loud so everyone can hear it, they complain about bills and how unhappy and unlucky life is. It is funny because I never really noticed this behavior they have always seemed to have before. I don't even know if it really bothers me because everyone around me seems to complain about everything, even me. So, I just made up the story and filled it with truths and memories because I do love my family. I got a D the teacher said it lacked feeling, whatever that was supposed to mean.

The second paper was supposed to be something we didn't like about ourselves and what we could do to change it. The idea was to see that we could grow and change and we do exactly that every day. I couldn't very well write that I hated myself for having sex or more accurately being raped at the age of ten, or about the shame and resentment I felt toward myself. So, I had to make something up and I said I didn't like the fact that I am not a very forgiving person and I should be because people deserve second chances. The teacher gave me a D and said that I didn't apply the effort I should have, she said the paper was boring like reading an encyclopedia page of cold hard facts, without detailed supporting reasons or testimony.

Then in health class when we started talking about our own bodies and how they work, then things turned into abstinence, I stopped participating. I didn't want to hear about my body or anyone else's body for that matter either. Then when I started my period in math class and had to ask to be excused; everyone saw the blood on my pants and starting talking about it and laughing at me. I felt so embarrassed, it was like time slowed down. I could feel all of their eyes on me and hear every whisper and laugh, I saw them pointing and the girls were doing it too. I didn't understand why all the girls were laughing and pointing, weren't they all dealing with the same thing every month too? So, I skipped math class for a week before I felt I could show my face again. That did not do anything good for my grade in that class.

A month after all the embarrassment in Math class I was walking to the elementary school to meet Will and walk him home. He stays in homework club after school until I get there to walk him home. I got this really strange feeling like someone was watching me or following me. I could hear the patter of feet behind me so I turned my head to look behind me. There were two guys with backpacks on behind me, they looked like maybe they were high school aged. I didn't think much of it and turned around and kept walking. It wasn't long before they started to shout things at me. They were taking turns shouting at me like some sick game.

"Hey you fine ass white girl"

"Didn't you hear my friend? Where are you walking to?"

"I would love to tap that ass?"

"Why don't you come sit on my face?"

"Yeah, Yeah Then you can sit that fine ass on my raging boner."

They continued to yell all these nasty things at me, even when I starting yelling for help. They just crossed the street and continued to smile as they yelled all their disgusting fantasies about what they wanted from me across the street. There was nobody home, nobody could hear my calls for help or they just didn't care. The faster I walked the faster they walked. I didn't start running until one of them yelled, "hey fuck this shit let's just rape that little cock tease!" I started running as fast as I could my feet pounding the pavement under them, my heart racing and sweat dripping from my face. They were chasing me still yelling behind me but I could not make out everything they were saying, all I could hear was my heart pounding and the blood pumping in my ears.

When I got to Los Cerritos Elementary school I burst into the main entrance and into the office. I fell to my knees and then laid on the floor crying as the staff members ran to help me up. When they took me to the principal's office my heart was still pounding and I was still crying so hard I could hardly breathe let alone talk; she gave me a few minutes to calm down so I could tell her what was going on. Once I was calm enough to talk, she hugged me and called my dad immediately. While we waited for my dad, she called the two closest local high school and had them bring photo binders of all their students.

When my dad got to the office he came in and she

filled him on what had happened, while I looked through the photos of the kids at the high schools. I found them both in the binders for the junior class at Millikan High. When the staff member wrote down their names and made copies of their photos and names for the police, I hoped they would be in trouble. My dad and the principal for the elementary school helped me talk to the police officers and make a report. Everyone was really supportive and seemed really concerned. The police officer told me that they take these things very seriously. Then he told my dad that because of my age, aside from my written testimony and the principals as a witness I wouldn't have to suffer the trauma of seeing the boys again. My dad said, "well I hope not she has been through enough!"

When we collected Will and left, I felt safe in the car being with my dad and brother, and I was reminded of how much I love my family and they love me. I could smell dad's cologne and it took me back to the days when I would sit in his lap and he would read me Put me in the Zoo or Go Dogs Go!

Dad took me to the store first and bought me a whistle to wear whenever I was walking by myself so I could blow it and people could hear it. Then we all went home and he showed me how to punch and how to defend myself in case I ever needed to. Will got into it too and it turned out to be pretty fun and it made me feel close to my family again. Then mom came home with some movies and pizza and we sat around watching movies while we ate. It was really nice to feel so close to my family and feel the safety net of their love and protection.

The school year has really flown by and I did my fair share of slacking off throughout the year. I felt it was more important to hang out with my friends talking about boys and shopping at the mall. I did buckle down though and pulled my grades to Bs so I am pretty proud of that. We also made a new friend and she had joined our circle of girls. She is real nice and kind of shy but she really comes out of her shell with us and she is pretty funny. She really likes to tell jokes and make people laugh and she is just about the nicest person ever. I can't for next year and all the fun we are going to have.

CHAPTER 13

STARTING OVER

Well we moved to Lakewood, so I have been going to Bancroft middle school since last year. Eighth grade is really exciting because it is the last year we have until high school. I really miss Jim and Tanner. I met them last year, they are one year ahead of me and really cool. It's funny because they are best friends but I can't decide which one I like more, although I really think it might be Jim.

It was so strange the way I met them because they just started showing up no matter where I was, and made it a point to talk to me. It made me really feel special but also weird. Plus, they always tell me how pretty I am and for the first time I really feel pretty. I am glad that mom started letting me wear makeup last year too, it helped boost my self confidence in a way I didn't know I needed. Makeup has really been becoming an art for me, and mom lets me wear it how I want as long as I don't use dark colors.

Everyday Jim and Tanner walk to my school to meet me and walk me home. It is nice that the high school gets out an entire hour earlier so they can do that. Jim always carries my book bag and folder for me, it really is such a kind thing to do. I can't wait until this school year is over so that I can join them in high school. Jim is so sweet I really feel like maybe we can be something more than just friends someday, even if he is afraid of my dad. It was so funny because Jim and Tanner were over the other day and we were talking on the lawn about our summer plans, and my dad came home from work; all he said was hi to me and I turned around and the guys were gone. They had left their bikes and just taken off. I thought it was pretty funny, but my dad didn't find it all that funny. He said that it seemed like they were up to no good if they felt like they needed to run off like that. I am not just going to believe that because I am sure it has something to with him telling them, "I have a shotgun, body bags and a shovel and doubt anyone will miss you, if you mess with my daughter!" What a great first introduction; clearly, he got his point across.

Well the last day of school was kind of cool but emotional. My friend Amy ran away from home, nobody would listen to her about her mom and her mom's boyfriend. They were really heavy into meth and beating her anytime she seemed in the way. Poor Amy would try to hide to change into her PE uniform; she always had welts and bruises all over her body and sometimes burns that she said came from cigarettes. She would not have food every day, which is why I used to give her my lunch. She said she was going to find her dad and I never saw her again. Then there was Julie, she was having sex with her high school boyfriend and got pregnant, her dad was so angry he beat her up pretty bad. I guess he just could not get over his anger because just one day before graduation we found out she shot herself. She just went in his room with his police work issued gun and shot herself while sitting on his side of the bed. I cried for her and for her mom; I could not imagine what her mom must be feeling since I was hurting so much, her mom must be devastated. She was such a beautiful person and I never knew suicide would be something I would have to hear about, let alone have to face the hurt personally of such a tragic loss.

Even though I want to be excited about graduating into high school, I feel guilty because of all the loss and sadness I feel in my heart. I keep wondering what ever happen to Amy, did she find her dad? And I kept thinking about Julie and wondered if she would have been excited today. This year has been really difficult and the loss of my friends stings; I just hope next year will be better. I hope I don't lose any more friends in such a permanent way again.

CHAPTER 14

BOY CRAZY

Summer break has been so much fun, I have been hanging out with Jim and Tanner a lot, but mostly Jim. He is handsome and I love the way he slicks his dirty blonde hair back, I bet he will be even more handsome when he gets his braces off. I go with him a lot to his football practices and wait for him so we can spend time together afterwards. Things have really been great between us and we just seem to click. I love cuddling with him while we watch movies or listen to music. He smells so good and I can't help but feel happy and loved.

I really wish I knew what is going on with Jim and I though....I mean are we a couple? Are we just friends? I don't know what the hell to think anymore, everything has gotten so complicated. We were kissing and making out on his bed in his room while we were watching tv. He had his hands up under my shirt but when he tried to get my pants off, I asked him to stop. He made me feel so guilty and asked me to give him a blowjob. I did it because I really like him and I wanted him to be happy with me. We seem a lot closer now, but I don't know what is going on. We hold hands and spend so much time together but then he turns around and starts flirting with other girls. I even saw him smack Katie on the ass today. It made me so angry but I just walked in the other direction to walk it off. I didn't want him to see me upset or know that I saw it or that it bothered me at all.

School started last week and I was really excited. Mom took me to buy all kinds of new clothes and makeup. We don't have to wear uniforms in high school so that is pretty exciting. My makeup skills are really coming along and mom has let me wear what I want in the makeup department; and I really do love applying it and playing with it. Jim and Tanner meet me at my house to walk me to school every morning. It makes me feel so important and special to be walking in with two of the most popular sophomores on the JV football team. They seem to know everybody or everybody knows them because they play football. The campus is so big, I was really intimidated at first that I would get lost and be late for classes. To my surprise though it didn't take me long to learn the campus lay out and navigate my way around.

Well the first month of school has been really interesting. Jim and I have recently had a falling out so to speak, and him and Tanner take my lunch every day. They just seem so different around their football buddies. I don't know what exactly is in the air in high school but it reeks of the immature musk of young dumb guys. They remind me of wild African animals. Always puffing up their chests, fighting and at times catching a whiff of a possible mating opportunity. YUCK!! Then once they get what they want or have an opportunity for commitment they hightail it on out of there in the other direction. They want to sleep with the girls around them, cuddle, be sweet and mushy when they are behind closed doors or alone with them, but they don't want to be seen that way in front of their friends. It's like teenaged boys lost a screw in their brains that tells them how to behave like decent human beings. Seeing Jim hug and kiss on other girls is not going to get to me. I mean who really cares, there are plenty of cute guys at this school anyway. Jim keeps trying to make me jealous talking to other girls in front of me, but staring at me the whole time; could he be any more obvious? It is not going to work on me, no way not this time. I know his games and won't fall into his trap again….DUCES!

I met these really cool guys, they are planning on going into the military after graduation so they are in the ROTC. They are both seniors and really fun to hang around. Tony has a car which is really awesome and Justin I have known for some time because he noticed me a few summers ago. But to be accepted into their group and to hang out with them is on another level of awesome. I mean they are seniors for crying out loud. My friend Carrie and I are going on a double date with them this weekend. It is going to be so much fun. Carrie is a sophomore and she knows so much about guys. She used to date a college guy so I trust her advice. She said if I really like a guy and want him to like me back, I should do what he wants to do and just enjoy myself. Maybe she is right and maybe I have been making a bigger deal out of sex then really should be made. Carrie also gave me some real helpful tips about sex, what to do and how to make it feel good for me and the guy. I am not so sure I am ready yet or that I can even think about who I would want to have sex with, but I will save those tips in the back of my mind.

Well things seem to be going really well, I have been seeing Tony and Carrie has been seeing Justin. We all went out to see Antz last weekend on a double date; I saved the movie stub because I wanted to remember how amazing the date was. Tony really dressed up in a nice shirt and slacks. He smelled so amazing with is Eternity for men cologne on. Tony bought us popcorn and drinks and then after the movie he bought me flowers at the flower stand in the town center. It was really so sweet, and he kept holding my hand and kissing me all night. I never thought I would like him so much but he is really sweet and so handsome. He has the best smile and he really does make me feel special; like I am the only girl in the world.

It looks like things are official now between Tony and I, he gave me his Senior jacket to wear. In high school that is the clear public sign that you are and item. He has a zero period before school so when he gets out of that class, he buys me hot chocolate at the student store and brings it over to me with a kiss. He also brings me little surprises every day, just like the other day when he hugged me and snuck a very little detailed yellow rose in a glass tube into the pocket of the jacket. I didn't know it was in there until I pushed my hands into the pockets because they were freezing cold. It really is all the little things that he does that make me fall more and more for him.

It has been three weeks and Tony said he can't stop touching me and all this making out is just making him want me more. I have been putting it off because I wasn't sure I am ready to have sex; maybe I should talk it over with him. I mean I think I love Tony and he says he loves me, so I think maybe it might be time. I will just call him now, "hi Tony, it's Gwen, I think we should talk."

"Shit babe sounds serious."

"Well for me it may be but maybe not so much for you. I have been thinking about how you brought up having sex and wanting me the other day. I need to know what you are feeling that tells you, you want this."

"I just love you babe, and we have been dating for a few weeks and you are so hot! Gosh just everything about you drives me crazy in all the right ways."

"I love you too Tony and I think I am ready to take our relationship to the next level. I just want it to be special."

After my conversation with Tony I feel so much better and more relaxed. I am actually glad that Carrie has been talking to me about all this too, she has really made me realize that I have just been being stupid and over thinking this. I am also excited because it will be the first time, I have sex consensually with someone it is also the first time I want to have sex at all. It is like I get to do my first time over. I have all these thoughts, worries and concern rolling around in my head. What if I do it wrong or chicken out completely? What if it feels disgusting or makes me feel dirty? No, it can't make me feel like that right; not when we both love each other.

Tony took me out on a date, just him and I. It was super romantic and nice, we saw the movie I had been waiting to see and then we went to dinner. He kept telling me how lucky he was to be with me and how beautiful I was. So, when we got back to his place, I was sure I was ready to have sex and he was the one. Thankfully he has his own private entrance to his room so his mom and stepdad don't know we are even here. Tony lit some candles and had a bottle of wine ready. I don't even like the way it tastes, but he said it would help me relax. He held my hand and then started kissing me, slowly he took my shirt off and then his. I felt so hot from the wine and nerves but I tried to push that thought out of my mind. He laid me down in his bed and took my heels off and started rubbing my legs and feet while I finished my wine. It was like a scene from a movie. Then Tony very carefully removed my panties from under my skirt, and I helped him with his pants. I can't believe I am doing this. Tony told me how much he loved me and I said thank you. Yep that is right I said thank you. Maybe he didn't notice because he laid me down and crawled on top of me. We were kissing each other and the heat of his body on mine was warm and comforting. He moved his mouth down to my breast and used his tongue to lick and tease my nipple blowing on it softly in between licks. Then he kissed me again as he brought his hand slowly up my thigh and gently messaged my clit and then he slipped his penis ever so gently inside me. As he was rocking his hips into me, he kept asking if I was ok. It was over fairly quickly and wasn't what I thought it be. Although it didn't hurt, there was no great pleasure or excitement for me, it was just kind of boring. He told me it would be better next time, I wasn't sure I wanted there to be a next time.

It has been a month since the first time I had sex with Tony, and it seems like that is how we spend so much of our time now. I think it is making me feel a bit used and a bit bitter or perhaps I am just becoming a bitch. Tony took me to the mall to go shopping today and I dropped my Lip Smackers vanilla bean roll on lip gloss. It rolled under the car and I made him get down on his hands and knees to get it. Then I threw it out because it landed on the nasty ground, and bless his heart he bought me a new one. I think that Tony is also starting to get really jealous of some of his friends. I don't know why because I am with him and who is he to tell me I can't talk to them? Ever since we started having sex things have just gotten weird and complicated. It is like we don't even talk anymore because all he wants to do is have sex, and to be honest it is still just as fast, boring and unpleasurable as it was the first time. I really wish I had the guts to tell him that…selfish prick!

I am really worried, I was supposed to start my period four days ago but I haven't yet. Carrie got me a pregnancy test which she brought to school to give me. She is such a good friend, she is going to go with me to Tony's house after school to be there with me when I take the test. Tony seemed really angry when I told him my period was late and now keeps saying really horrible stuff to me. He called me a whore and told me I must have been with someone else. No matter how many times I tell him that isn't true he just does not seem to be able to let it go. He acts like he isn't half the reason I even have to take a pregnancy test in the first place.

At least Tony was there holding my hand while we waited for the test results to be ready. It was the longest five minutes of my life. It came back positive and I can't stop crying, how am I going to tell my parents. How am I going to raise a baby? I am only fourteen years old I shouldn't be having to ask myself these questions. I guess Tony is going to think of a way out of this. He said he loves me too much to let me go through this alone.

What a jerk, just yesterday Tony said he would be there for me and today he is already prowling around on some other girl. His ex-girlfriend also found me to tell me what a cheater he is. She told me that he went and cheated on me last week with the same girl he cheated on her with. She said that he called and told her everything because he was feeling guilty about it. I can't believe that with everything that is going on that sex would be what he is so worried about right now. Oh well, I hope it was worth it because I never want to see him again. Only what am I supposed to do about this baby? I can't be a single mother, I am so scared. I see the other girls at school that are pregnant and people are so mean to them. The guys laugh and push them or throw things at them and the girls all whisper behind their backs and give them judgmental looks as they walk by. I don't understand it because the human race would not exist without sex for procreation. We are all doing it…having sex with our boyfriends and girlfriends, it could happen to anyone of us. It did to me…

Stress is a serious thing, I have been so upset that Tony keeps blowing me off and ignoring me. I mean seriously after getting me pregnant, then this prick was cheating on me; now he is just going to turn his back on me and shut me out. I am just so sick with worry and stress, it all boils down to Tony as the cause of it all. I started bleeding during gym class today; a big part of me feels happy about that. I got blood on my gym shorts but I was too happy to care and nobody laughed or made any immature comments this time, because by now every girl has started having periods. I got an off campus pass to walk to Planned Parenthood before school gets out. Thank God Carrie told me they have to allow it. I went in to get checked out just to be safe and they said I lost the pregnancy. I guess this happens on its own all the time. I told them how stressed out I have been and they said it could have contributed to the miscarriage. At least now I don't have to tell my parents or be a single teenaged mother.

It has been about two months since the miscarriage and I feel better. Tony and I say hi if we see each other in the halls. I am still friendly with his group of friends too but I am so over him. I met a new guy at the mall last week with Carrie. He is the manager at Lids hat shop in the mall. He came out of the store to talk to me when he saw me walking by, he was so cool. He is twenty-nine years old and I will be fifteen in a month so it is cool. I am so close to being an adult woman now and I am so mature for my age anyway. I have been meeting him every day for lunch, and today my parents said they want to meet him. He seemed really nervous when I told him about meeting my parents, and said we should tell them he is twenty, so that is what we are going to do. I don't know how I feel about lying to them or why he is asking me to, but he must have his reasons.

My parents are so horrible they hate Rob, the new guy I have been seeing. Mom said she doesn't want me dating someone that old, but she is just being unreasonable. I don't care what she says we are going to the movies tonight so hopefully she can just get over it.

Rob and went back to his place after the movie and had sex. It was so much better than with some lame high school guy. There was that moment of pleasure and it was so great, sex wasn't so boring after all. He really loves me I know it. He gets a little jealous whenever he sees me talking to Jim and Tanner but he needs to get over it, they are my friends. Besides this week is the winter formal and he is going with me. I bought our tickets already.

Rob hated being around all my friends, most of the guys kept saying how weird he is for being with me. It is just because they are jealous. So, we left and went to his house to have sex. After we had sex, we came back to go meet my friends at Denny's after the dance, and I don't know what happened. Jim gave me a hug and Rob was so upset about it he grabbed me by the arm really hard and dragged me inside. He told me I was embarrassing him, that I was his and should not be hugging other guys. It scared me at first, but he just loves me too much. I guess he is afraid I will breakup with him is all. We are going to see The Cure tomorrow, they are playing at Irvine Meadows, I am so excited.

The concert would have been so much better if I went by myself. The entire time Rob was yanking me around because guys were talking to me or looking at me. He got so mad when he thought I was looking at some other guys that he yelled at me. When we got in the car after the concert, he just started yelling at me and hitting me. I couldn't believe it. After these past few months together I never thought he would hit me, but he did. Maybe he is hitting me and so volatile because of the drugs I have recently seen in car. That baggie of powder is not just in his ashtray because he is throwing it out, he was hiding it from me.

Today Rob took me to the Korn meet and greet because I love Korn. But I don't ever want to see him again. He got so jealous because of the way he said I was looking at Jonathan Davis, that he put his hands around my throat and starting choking me as soon as we got back in the car. I was clawing at him for him to stop, but then suddenly he just started punching me. The pain as each blow hit me was so extreme and the sound of the blows in my head made my stomach turn. I am going to have to hide out from mom and dad and up my makeup game to hide the bruises.

I really feel bad about avoiding my parents and covering my bruised-up face with makeup. Mom noticed a few bruises on my face and I told her PE has been really rough on me because I suck at baseball. She bought it I think, but I feel horrible having to lie to her. It will never have to happen again though because I broke things off with Rob.

CHAPTER 15

HIGH SCHOOL WARS

School has gotten to be a little scary and strange. I don't feel safe there and I am always looking over my shoulder, I can feel the tension in the air. It is as if there is something in the water that the staff and students ingested that made their brains go haywire. Most of the kids have formed groups gathering by ethnicity, they spit racial slurs at one another and it is heartbreaking to me. I wish they weren't so ignorant and could just see that we are human, we all bleed and if you turned us all inside out there is no difference. It does not matter what the pigment in your skin or the color of your eyes or hair we are really the same. The violence and fights have become so common, and so threatening to the lives of so many of those involved as well as the students like me who want nothing to do with hate are impacted. All of the girls bathrooms are locked and we have to let a staff member know if we have to use the restrooms. The only bathrooms that are not locked are the eight hundred building bathrooms and that is because there is a staff member that stands outside them while they are unlocked. This decision was made after three girls were jumped, cut up and stabbed in the bathrooms. One of those victims was injured so badly she bled out in the bathroom in the two hundred building. The school has not made any official announcements because they don't want panic or the public to get wind of it. I only know about it because I didn't feel well last week and while I was waiting for mom to pick me up, I was listening in on conversations between staff in the office. Their hush tones and the over the shoulder glances really spiked my curiosity and ability to hone in my listening skills. The staff is afraid of many of the students but at the same time are pushing back, it just seems to make everything more volatile. A few teachers have taken on the behavior of these ignorant teens. They will scream and shout spewing foul language at any student that puts one toe out of line….it was a verbal powder keg.

The school has been working with the local law enforcement trying to gain control over the students, and trying to track down weapons and drugs. They bring in dogs and do random backpack checks. I had a lighter on me that I use for my kohl eyeliner, heating it up just helps it glide on easier. When they searched my makeup bag, they tried to take it, but I am so obsessed with makeup and my appearance I protested and got sent to my administrator. I told him along with the campus officer that I had never caused any problems nor do I smoke or use drugs, that it was simply for my eyeliner and I showed them what I was talking about. They both decided to allow me to keep my lighter as long as I didn't tell anybody, and because they didn't feel I was threat. It was a relief that I had won that battle and I was glad they could see my side of things.

I guess one of the students tried to smuggle a sheet of acid around the backpack searches. He tucked it under his belt and shirt. When the heat of the day kicked in and he started sweating it didn't end well. His skin had absorbed so much of the acid that he overdosed and the paramedics had to come for him. I hear that they got to him in time and that he is going to survive with medical intervention, but it is unclear at this point if he will be the same. There is concern that the acid may have caused permanent damage to his brain.

I am so thankful that my first year of high school is over. It really was a rougher ride than I thought it would be. Summer has been relaxing and I have been spending time at the beach with friends or inside reading. I have also gone to the mall quite a bit. I love shopping and have found some pretty cool shorts at Miller's Outpost, I like them so much I am going to go get two more pairs. I also finally bought the Britney Spears CD. I mostly listen to metal and rock but I tend to like a little of everything, so I don't care what people say. Music has also been one of those things that I don't care what anyone says, if I like it....I like it. Music has always been a way for me to escape, or tie with a memory or feeling. It is like the music really speaks to me.

CHAPTER 16

DEBATING THE FUTURE

Well time has been flying by for me. Not too much happened sophomore or junior year for me. In fact, aside from a relationship blooming between myself and Will's best friend Trevor nothing very exciting happened. I was probably more shocked than anybody that it was even a possibility for me to be into Trevor. He is a year younger than me and a year older than Will and he lives a few houses down from us. I remember in middle school if he saw me and said hi, how I used to just look at him from the corner of my eye and keep walking. If my friends asked who he was I would tell them I had no idea, I had never seen him before in my life. But he has really grown up and he is so damn hot all of the sudden. Everything between Trevor and I started over summer. He started sneaking into my bedroom window and we would watch movies on the tv in my room while we cuddled. Then one night we started kissing and somehow that ended up turning into us having sex. We were having sex all summer before sophomore year. About two months into the new school year that followed. I told him it was getting to hard for me because I loved him and he didn't feel the same. When he kissed me and told me that he loved me too, I was so happy.

On campus we don't talk, I can't even be seen with him. He hangs around with the slackers by the elevators and I don't want my friends to give me shit, I also don't want to collect the stigma from the staff members. It makes it more fun that way anyway.

Other than the relationship between Trevor and I, high school was pretty relaxed until senior year. And us keeping our relationship a secret has been going so well not even my dad or Will are aware. Mom knows but that is just because she isn't stupid and plus, we talk.

So, what has been going on senior year that has jumbled my relaxed going with the flow vibe? Well right from the first day of school there was trouble. I got my class schedule and saw two classes I have already taken on it, so I had to try to get that fixed. My senior guidance counselor is horrible though and notoriously known through the student body of being racial. She favors the African American kids; which seems so pigheaded and childish considering her age and it is 2001 by the way, we should be past all that nonsense. I walk into her office after knocking on the door and explain my situation to her and ask her if she can fix it. This bitch looked me dead in the face and told me, you will just have to stay in the classes you have but you won't be getting credit if you have already taken them. I was so angry I asked her to change my elective because I already took draw and paint and all the other art classes were full. I suggested she change that class to auto mechanics. She laughed and said you are a girl you can't take auto mechanics. I didn't understand why my gender defined my ability to be able to fix a car but I was really getting upset. Then she told me the math and English classes were full and so she couldn't fix the mistakes in those classes being on my schedule. Then she told me we are done here as she smiled and motioned for a pretty black cheerleader to come in so she could fix her issues. When I was walking out and heard the counselor say she would do whatever it takes to get her class changed I lost my shit. I yelled at her for being racial and having it out for me because I am a white girl and her wanting to keep me down. I told her how disgusted I was with her behavior and how much she shouldn't be working with people period, let along young people working toward their future. She laughed and rolled her eyes.

I stomped over to the Secretary desk and asked one of the secretaries for a transfer paper. They asked which type of transfer and I told them schools. They didn't look too surprised considering they heard me yell at the guidance counselor. I got the paper and walked over to my administrator's door that was open just a crack and I kicked it open. I stormed in, "what's up buttercup?" he asked.

"Oh, nothing just needed a place to sit while I fill out this paper to transfer schools!"

I read and spoke everything I was filling in out loud to

make sure he knew I meant business.

"Name: Guinevere Elizabeth Collins, transferring from: Lakewood High, School of choice: Millikan High."

His face was just frozen for a minute, like he didn't know what was going or what to expect. I know he had to have heard some kind of commotion when I was yelling at my guidance counselor. I just carried on as I was filling out the paper work writing and reading it and speaking my responses out loud.

"Reason for transfer: Racial discrimination."

At this my administrator jumped up and told me to calm down, that all this wasn't necessary. He asked me what was going on and I explained the situation. He fixed my schedule and changed my problem classes, for English though he gave me speech and debate. He told me that over all the years he had known me, that he expected I would excel and have nothing less than and easy A in that class. From then on, he told me that the senior guidance counselor was not allowed to deal with my classes or any other issue I was having, he would deal with me directly. I walked out of his office laughing at the fact that they still want to refer to the senior counselor with guidance in her job title. Well just because they want to buy into that belief I wasn't going to hop on that bandwagon, nope not today Satan! I had her number, I knew exactly what she was, a snake in the grass with a mind washed in hate and discrimination. The whole time I was telling her what I thought she never even denied any of it, she just nodded and smiled.

CHAPTER 17

INAPPROPRIATE TEACHER

I am really glad that first semester is over and I am done with government, and onto a new class and teacher in economics. It wasn't even the material that I hated so much, it was all the weirdness that me uncomfortable.

First off, the teacher Mr. Woods was such a dorky creeper. He just graduated from college with his teaching credentials and is twenty-four years old and probably shouldn't be teaching at a high school, maybe elementary would be more appropriate; considering how close the age gap is between him and the students. I had his class right after my lunch period and I would normally be the first one in, he would always greet me by saying, "hi beautiful!" At first, I thought he was just being nice, but things got really uncomfortable when he starting telling how beautiful I looked every day and asking me what I like to do in my free time, he even asked if I had a boyfriend. It all just made me so uncomfortable, not necessarily because of his age but because he was my teacher and I knew it was wrong. It also didn't help that I didn't find him attractive. He was not very manly to me for his age and was almost weasley to me. Then when he started walking through the class when we were quietly working on our class assignments, he would put his hand on my shoulder and rub it or squeeze it; I could feel the icy chill or discomfort roll down my spine. When I had to do the baby project for health class and I had to carry around a ten pound doll twenty-four hours a day for two weeks, he made that more uncomfortable than it needed to be as well. He would carry my doll around and say creepy things like, "why didn't you tell me we were expecting a baby." Or, "I can watch our baby while you do your work, I want you to succeed." It was just all so wrong, but he really crossed the line when the semester was over and he called my house. He asked to speak with my mom so I naturally thought I was in some kind of trouble. That was not what he was calling about at all. He had the audacity to ask my mom if he could take me out for coffee. I never heard my mom yell at anyone the way she yelled at Mr. Woods. Sure, I was nearly eighteen but that didn't change the way mom stood up for me and my well-being.

On top of the teacher being a complete creeper there were two boys in my class that period that really gave me the heebeegeebees. First there was Bobby who would just flat out stare at me the whole class. No matter where I was or what I was doing he was always watching and staring. If I was finished with my work and got up to turn it in, he was watching. If I was working quietly, he was watching. If Mr. Woods was talking to the class he was watching. It was so bad that when the teacher would call on him to interject, he never had a clue as to what was going on or what we were doing in class.

Then there was James, he was a whole other head case. I have quite the shoe collection and I wear what goes best with what I choose to dress myself in. So, strappy shoes opened toed pumps and flats are all a part of my wardrobe. James sits right to the left of me so when he saw my feet and toes, he really started talking to me about them. He asked me if he can rub my feet and suck on my toes, which is just weird. If I wore Chuck Taylor's, Adidas shoes or even boots, he would pay me to take my shoes off in class. I mean hey, if I had to sit through this class with all these weirdos I may as well make a little money right. Plus, I could use the extra twenty dollars a day to add to my mall shopping funds.

Trevor and I also decided to take a break from each other for a while. He has been doing nothing but smoking weed and partying and I didn't know if that is a person I want to really be with. Hopefully he cuts back and starts getting it together. I mean everyone smokes a little weed here and there or at least tries it, even I did. I got a little lit between class two weeks ago to help me relax because we had a huge test and I was a mess because it was a weighted test. Luckily for me when I walked into that science class there was a substitute teacher and the test was postponed. We ended up watching a National Geographic film on hyenas. When the narrator said they thought in the past that hyenas were asexual, due to the fact that both males and females have long extended penises that they used to drag on the brush and grass to mark it; I straight fell back out of my chair laughing. I slapped the desk picking myself up off the floor and said, "Oh my God rewind that shit, did he seriously just say that funny ass shit?" It awarded me a trip to my administrator with a referral. When I got to his office, I was still laughing so hard I could hardly tell him what was so funny. He just ripped up my referral and sent me to sit on his bench until next period. I guess he just let it go since I have never been in trouble before.

CHAPTER 18

ABSENCE OF MORALITY

Life just seems to have this way of escaping me in a way that I haven't even noticed how fast time goes by. After the stress of turning eighteen and becoming a legal adult making it real, meaning if I mess up now, I can get in deep legal trouble, had passed things got easy again. I am getting ready for graduation and I don't know how I feel about that. All my friends have plans that seem more solid than mine. I am going to Long Beach City College after graduation but some of my friends are going into the military or off to universities. I spent most of second semester in a long-distance relationship with Justin. He came home for a visit and we spent the whole time together, we just really clicked. I was planning on getting married to Justin for a short time. He has been in the Army since after he graduated three years ago. But after 9/11 he was deployed, and every time he called he seemed rushed to get married. He wanted me to drop out of school to move to Georgia and marry him, I just can't do that. So, I had to break it off! Now I am back with Trevor and things are better than before.

I had an end of the year project due for economics class Monday, so I waited all day on Saturday for my friend and project partner Dean to show up so we could work together to finish it. I had already done most of the work so I wasn't too worried that he was late. Then mom came into my room as I was working on the project, and gave me the article that said that Dean was a victim of a shooting at a party on Friday night. I new about the party and the all the drama that went down because Will was there. When mom and dad found him safe and well, they grounded him for a month. They will let him off early I am sure with good behavior but they had a point, he had no business sneaking off to the party. Will told me about the shooting; apparently it occurred after some fight broke out over whether or not the Lakers were the best basketball team in the league. Our friend Joey took a bullet in the hand and arm trying to get over the wall in the back of the house. Dean didn't get to wall in time, I guess. My economics teacher took my project complete as is and didn't force me to complete Deans portion of it. It was really nice of her because I was struggling with the loss of a friend. He was silly and fun, really just a class clown. The worst part of all it was when our class broke off into groups to collect donations to help pay for Dean's funeral expenses. Mr. Woods said he didn't feel sorry for him and wouldn't donate a penny. This callus ass hat actually tried to bribe me to go to dinner with him for a donation. He was claiming my friend who I was mourning was nothing more than a fuck up that deserved what he got. I was disgusted, hurt and completely pissed off that anyone could say that about another human being. It was as if his life didn't matter so it wasn't something to worry about in the eyes of Mr. Woods. That teacher is just a warped creep without actual morality.

CHAPTER 19

THE END OF A CHAPTER

Graduation was miserable, I went surfing a few days before and got sick from the bacteria in the water. I should have known better because of the storm that blew in off shore the night prior, I mean I have been a surfer and beach goer all of my life. I just wasn't thinking of anything more than the salty sea air and the waves. I loved surfing, no matter what was going on in my life or how stressed I felt it just all wash away with the water. I never felt freer than when I was surfing and it brought me a little closer to God when I was in that water, because I was truly in God hands. I just wish I would have thought twice because I was so sick through the graduation ceremony that I could hard sit through it or walk across the stage for my diploma.

When I got home after the ceremony, Trevor ran me a nice hot bath with lavender Himalayan bath salts. As he helped me into the tub I let the, lavender smell envelop me and relax away my body aches. When I was out of the bath Trevor rubbed my back to make me feel completely calm and relaxed, to help me feel better. He has been staying over for the past few weeks and I really love that he was here with me. I just know that Trevor is it for me. He is so handsome in a manly way and I love every single second we have together. We just know each other so well and it is so comfortable.

My heart is shattered into a million pieces. Trevor went on a trip with Will to Washington and cheated on me with some little thirteen-year-old girl. What was he thinking? He shouldn't be messing around with a girl that young he is seventeen. What makes matters worse is he thought I wouldn't find out? I get that he probably thought it was no big deal because guy code and my brother being his best friend; but come on of course Will told me, blood comes before friends. It is not like I haven't done everything for him and it's not like we don't have sex because we do, all the time. I really thought all the love and passion between us was real. He keeps trying to call and come by but I just don't want to see him right now, he really hurt me.

After two weeks of blowing Trevor off I finally agreed to let him come in and talk to me. He brought me a huge arrangement of flowers and a beautiful gold bracelet that he worked so hard for. I don't know why I love him so much after how he betrayed me and hurt me so deeply.. But we talked things through and it felt really therapeutic. Trevor said, "I am so sorry I hurt you like that baby, I love you and I wasn't thinking. I had too much to drink and it just happened."

"It just happened Trevor? How stupid do you think I am? You fucked up and you need to be a man about it."

"You are so right baby, I really fucked up and now I am terrified I am losing you forever, please don't do this to me, to us."

"Do what to us, you are the one that whipped your out cock the first second you thought you could get it wet and cheated. You really broke my heart, I trusted you."

"I know all that baby and I am sorry, it will never happen again. It didn't mean anything anyway she was just sex. I have only ever loved you and I am in love you."

"I guess we have been through a lot and I do love your stupid ass, so I am sorry too. I forgive you jerk face."

We just stood there kissing and for so long, and then we ended up having the most amazing makeup sex. I really wish I would have thought to lock the door, because mom walked in on us. We had a box of condoms out all kinds of different lubricants and sex toys and we were just going at it like jackrabbits, it was so humiliating. She just said sorry then she quietly closed the door. After our two rounds of makeup sex we had a good laugh about mom walking in. I mean I kind of don't care because I am eighteen after all. I just wish we weren't caught in the act and spared the humiliation of eye contact.

After a year of happiness, love and joy; I have to

end things with Trevor. I love him I really do, but it has also been a struggle. I am working and going to school struggling to carve out a future for myself, and all he cares about is partying and doing drugs. I am so sick of having to drag him to the shower after he gets home covered in vomit or wondering what time he will be back. It just isn't fair when I am working so hard and he is having the time of his life. I really wish he would just grow up already and start getting serious about school or maybe join the military. He is eighteen and perhaps with all his slacking off in school the military might be the best option for Trevor at this point.

I recently just found out through one of Trevor's friends that has been cheating on me with different girls for the past month. How could he be doing this to me again? He was at school because he is very close to the end of his senior year and he was supposed to be in the study hall. Instead I found him hanging out under the bleachers with some skank claiming they were just watching the baseball tryouts. Watching tryouts my ass; I saw them kissing, they were all over each other. To make matters worse I knew this skank and she was one of the easiest girls in his class. Last year I was glad to be getting away from high school girls like her because they cause trouble, I never thought I would be confronting her now. When I asked how being all over each other kissing was watching tryouts they both lied to me. In a fit of rage, I grabbed a baseball that had been left by the supply room door under the bleachers, and I beat her with it. I hit her until she was covered in bruises and bleeding. When I snapped out of my rage, I felt awful but I still threatened her that snitches wind up in ditches and then walked away. I ignored Trevor and told him we were over for good and pushed past him to get home. I am not going to keep putting up with this, and clearly, I was no longer some weak, soft little cry baby anymore.

When I broke things off with Trevor he was pretty upset. I felt horrible but he needs to get sober and keep his penis in his pants. I felt stupid for giving him the chance to hurt me again, pushing me mentally and emotionally to a place I had never known I had in me. I felt awful for beating up that skank, Tina. I mean what do I care who she sleeps with, and she did me a favor if I really think about it, by allowing me the opportunity to catch Trevor in the act.

My period is two weeks late so I had better get my but over to Planned Parenthood. I really hope that when that condom broke it was nothing and I have nothing to worry about. I am praying that I am just late because stress is throwing my cycle off. I haven't been feeling so good though the past few days so I am a bit more concerned.

Well I am pregnant with Trevor's baby. The problem is, I had to schedule an appointment for an abortion. It seems that the embryo doesn't look right, which may be because of Trevor's drug use. I am not sure but I can't have a baby that won't have a good quality of life or worse that could die after birth. When the doctor told me. I was in fact pregnant it hadn't really sunk in yet, when the next thing he said was, something is wrong. He looked at the ultrasound screen really closely and told me that since I was actually eight weeks pregnant the heartbeat should regularly beat in rhythm, but it seems to be skipping. My mind could not grasp what he was actually saying. He said that he recommends termination due to the father's history of drug use. He also told me but that they would do a scan before the procedure to ensure that it was still the right option.

I told Trevor what was going on, but he has already latched onto some new girl. I have been dealing with the weight of this whole situation on my own and these past two weeks have been hell emotionally. It must be nice to not have to deal with or face the messes you create like Trevor seems to continue to do. Coasting through life fuck up after fuck up with no real worries because mommy is always there to clean up your messes.

As I am laying on this clinic table I am crying for me and crying for my baby, because I am afraid that there is no other option and I haven't even had time to process everything. When the doctor comes in the nurse helps calm me and tells me they are going to do an ultra sound first to make sure there is error as she pushes the ultra sound machine closer to the table. During the second scan the doctor tells me that the heart is skipping and that the embryo looks abnormal; that if carried to term the baby would die within hours after birth. I cried and agree to go through with the abortion and signed the paper work. The nurse talked to me and told me that I am doing what is best for my baby given the circumstances. I know deep down that she is right but it does not make it any easier, my heart is shattering. I never even had choice about the life growing inside of me and now I already have to say goodbye.

After spending some time dealing with all the pain surrounding the hardest choice I ever had to make, I am feeling better. I crumbled alone in my room and wore a mask when around everyone else, I couldn't tell anyone. What would they think of me for getting pregnant, would they even believe me that the condom broke or that the baby wasn't healthy? I just want to keep it between me and God; God knows my heart and knows how hard that was for me. When I see all the people picketing or passing out unsolicited advice and opinions on abortion, I want to scream at them to shut up. They have no place to judge any of those women, they don't know their story, their reasons or their heart. They don't know how difficult that choice really is and what it does to a mother. I was really upset when just a month after my abortion, another girl was leaving a womens clinic and an anti-abortion extremist shot the young teen in the back and killed her. She was just there to have a pap and get the pill, and if life matters so much to these people why didn't hers? Going to church and praying have helped me so much, I know that I had no real choice. Trevor has moved on and we are still friends I guess, but I try to stay away when he comes to hang out with Will and his girlfriend. I really hate Will's girlfriend she is such a nasty bitch so it makes avoiding Trevor really easy. I guess I can move on from Trevor now since I was able to just let it all go and pray through my pain.

CHAPTER 20

CYBER HUNTER

I have been talking to this guy Paul on Myspace for a few weeks now. We are supposed to meet up for coffee and surfing. It should be fun. It is so strange because I am getting ready for my date with Paul but for no reason, I have a bad feeling in the pit of my stomach. I am sure it will pass. I better get on the road before I am late.

Paul is really cute and so far, he seems really nice. We met for coffee and we were supposed to go surfing, but he said that his roommate is throwing a pool party at their place and asked if I wanted to that instead. I figured that since other people will be there it should be fine.

Wow there are so many people at this party, Paul said I can change in the bathroom in his room. When I came back down the music was turned down and everyone was gone. I don't understand maybe we were too late and maybe I should go. But Paul pulls on my hand and convinces me to go to the pool with him. The pool has a gate around it and a lock on it that needs a key to get in or out of the pool. I guess since it is an apartment complex pool it makes it safer that way. Paul pored a wine cooler into a glass for me, I don't want to drink though because I have to drive home, but he is really insisting.

So, I took one drink and now everything seems to be in a fog and I feel funny. Paul is pushing himself on me and kissing me really hard and I don't like it. He told me he didn't want to have sex with me and I could not help but respond, "well who offered to have sex with you?" What a jerk I had no intention of having sex with him, I don't even know him. Then he told me that I was sexy and he had hormones like a raging bull, whatever that means. After what seemed like an eternity, I made an excuse to go to the restroom that was in the pool area. There was really something wrong, something wrong with him and something wrong with me, I wasn't feeling right and my brain was all hazy and I felt like I was running low on energy. I splashed my face with water to try to wake myself up and wash away the sudden funk that had settled over me and felt like I might vomit. I left the water running so I could think; how was I going to get away from this creep. On no... Paul is pounding on the door wondering what is taking me, so long. "I just feel a little sick." I say. When I open the door, he is right there. I feel as if my legs have turned to jello.

When we get back to his apartment, I go to his room to change. My legs are suddenly numb now and I fall to the floor by the bed. As I struggle to get up, Paul comes into the room naked. I immediately start to cry, begging him to let me go and not hurt me. Paul stays silent and picks me up and throws me on the bed then he climbs on top of me. I can see and talk but I can't move my body, it is as if I am trapped in my own body. Paul unties my bikini top and mentions how huge and perfect my tits are as he stars licking and biting them all over. The pain from his bites sinking into my breasts send more tears to fall down my face, and I know now that I am in real danger. I start screaming for help and crying, so his roommate comes in and turns up the stereo to drown out my pleas for help. As I am begging him to just let me go, Paul cuts off my bikini bottoms, which scares me and angers me because it is my favorite swim suit. Then with the knife he used to cut off my bottom he puts it inside me and bites my right breast as hard as he can. He then moved down to bite and lick my vagina and lap up all the blood from the fresh wounds his knife and teeth have created. I am trying not to focus on the pain or the fear and I am praying for my life while fighting the urge of passing out, what did he put in my drink? Then he pulls the knife out of me and slips his penis inside me and starts really driving himself into me as if he is enjoying all of this. I start to disconnect from my body and I start to have flash backs of camp and Matt all those years ago. All I do is pray his does not kill me; I can get out of this, I am a fighter. Every inch of me is struck by a fear I have never felt and I am praying for my life harder than I have ever prayed for anything. Then suddenly as he is raping me and biting me, I thank God for giving me the strength to escape this evil man, and I gather enough strength to sucker punch him off of me. I run to the bathroom and I lock the door, then I slip in my own blood and hitting my head.

When I come to, I can hear Paul and his roommate banging on the door. So, I get dressed and grab my purse; thank goodness I left it in here when I changed earlier. Then I listen with my ear pressed to the door, I wait until I hear them walk out of the room. Then I open the door and run like I have never run before. Once I get outside, I start screaming for help all the way to my car. Paul is chasing me, buck naked and not one person comes out to see what all the commotion is about or to save me. "What is wrong with people?" I make it to my car and get in as fast as I can locking the doors I start the car and I back out so fast I nearly hit Paul. I don't care I need to get away fast. My tires screech as I speed away, I can feel the adrenaline melting away slowly. I get on the 405 and then get off two exits away and call everyone in my phone, until a friend picks up. I am amazed I got as far as I did because my body felt like jelly and my brain was still in a fog. My friend Zack came and drove my car; first back to Paul's even though I protested against it. He planned on beating the crap out of him I guess, but Paul wasn't answering the door. Then we headed to the Costa Mesa police department, I had to stop first to pee; and walking into that Denny's, I felt like a freak show. Everyone was staring at me and I didn't know why until I got to the bathroom. My hair was a mess and I was covered in blood, I can only image what they were thinking.

When we made it to the police station I became completely upset. The Kobe Bryant rape scandal had been all over the media and I guess that made the cops act like the pig-headed idiots they are. They told me I wanted it to happen. They said that because I wore a dress and then a bikini that I was begging for it. It crippled me to tears, who says something like that? No, I didn't want it, and no I most certainly didn't want to be cut up and have bruises and bites all over me. And NO way in hell, did I want that nasty penis inside me at any time.

I was thankful that they had to take me to the hospital, I was sick of looking at these police men with no damn sense in their heads. At the rape unit in the hospital a support sponsor showed up. When she got here, the sponsor really helped calm me down and she yelled at the officer for being so cold, callus and ignorant. Then she told me she knows what I was going through because she was a victim of rape too. It made me feel not so alone and a little bit safer, even if I don't know why.

My phone won't stop, Paul keeps texting me threatening me not to tell and also pleading with me to tell him where I am. The officer takes notes and pictures of all the texts. Then I go in for my exam better known as a rape kit, they clean and swab all my body for DNA and tell me that the damage will heal. Then they give me medications just in case he had any STDs so that I don't get it. Then they collect my bikini top and the panties I have on for evidence. It all scares me even more and I just never want to see another man in all my life. I feel dirty and completely broken.

As soon as I got home, I took the hottest shower I could and scrubbed my body until my skin was sore and raw. There was so much blood it took a while for the water to run clear. Why does this shit always happen to me? Why does God hate me so much? What did I do to deserve this? I will just focus on school from now, that way when I turn 20 in a month, I can afford to take a day away from studies.

A month later I get a call from a detective that was working on my case, she tells me they have arrested Paul and that there is more good news. She told me that when they served a search warrant for his apartment, they found my bikini bottoms and traces of my blood in the apartment. She also told me that he denied any knowledge of his roommate being involved but that he just confessed to assault and rape charges. He told them that he did rape me and that he did cut me up and that if he ever saw me again, he would finish what he started. So, they feel it is in my best interest of safety to have the DA stand in when his trial starts. He has to go to trial because they linked him to four missing women and three rape and murder victims, through his Myspace account and DNA. She said that the judge declared him as a danger to society and denied his bail. I finally feel safe and it feels good to know that he can't hurt anybody else.

CHAPTER 21

LOST IN ENVY

"Gosh Gwen, where is your life headed?" I can't stop asking myself that question. As I sit alone on the sand in the dark at the beach, I let my mind reflect on the past. Feeling the damp sand under my bottom as I dig my toes into the sand I take in deep breaths of sea air. I feel calm listening to the waves and watching them crash on the shore, and I think about God.

With everything I have been through is it really God's fault? Did God perfect the scenes of my life like he did with Christ? Is that really how that worked, or was Christ just accepting of the fate he knew he would face for telling the people the truth? Maybe nothing was really God's fault at all, maybe it was everyone else's fault that had a part in hurting me. Did God really create so many bad people?

The more I thought the more confused I made myself. Nothing made since to me, life was really painful and such a struggle.

Maybe I was really messing up in life and making all the wrong choices. The only problem is sometimes I never even had a say or a choice. So, why is it that God won't listen to me? What do I have to do for God to help me? Maybe I am being a little harsh on God right now because I am certain that God heard me praying and helped me escape Paul. I mean the rape kit results came back and the detective told me GHB usually passes through the system so quickly it goes undetected. She also told me that he gave me so much that they not only picked up high levels of it in my blood, but they were surprised I was even able to save myself or stay awake. So, did God have a hand in that?

I just want to find a healthy balance in my life. I mean I am sure things I don't like may happen but why can't the good out way the bad? What am I doing wrong?

I think about all my friends and I feel jealous. I envy them for being able to go to expensive schools, drive nice cars and have happy relationships. Some of my friends are planning weddings and honeymoons, others are traveling around the world on their down time. While I am just a lame sad little Gwen, kicking rocks and wishing I had it so easy. I dream about seeing the world and being in a happy relationship, but those things don't seem to be in the cards for me, at least not now.

"I don't know what the future holds for me but I really hope you have something better in the works for me

God!"

CHAPTER 22

JOSHUWA

I never thought I would ever feel ok again after being raped especially around men. But it has been almost a year and I am ok. I have made all kinds of friends through Myspace which is cool, because otherwise I would be too busy to meet new people because of school. I think that I might want to work with the FBI or something in law enforcement. Just think the headlines could read "FBI Agent Collins Caught The Most Wanted Pedophile" one day. I would be just like a superhero and it would be so fulfilling. Ok I admit that is a little bit cheesy, especially for someone who lives in a huge city in California and not some small town in the boon docks somewhere.

I am going to go on a date with this really cool guy. He is about fourteen years older than me, he has kids with his ex-wife, but still he is really great. We have been talking for a while and he makes me laugh and smile which counts for something. He is so hot too, he has black hair that he slicks back and he is covered in tattoos. He has that greaser, rockabilly style and I love it. His name is Joshuwa, and I really like the way he spells his name it is so unique.

The night of our first date, Joshuwa picked me up and took me to dinner at Black Angus. At first, I teased him a little because he is about an inch shorter than me. I am five foot seven and a half inches tall but I have always been with men taller than me. So, when he pulled up in his BMW and got out to open my door for me, I jokingly said, "no really where is my real date?" We both laughed because it broke the first date ice. It doesn't matter to me how tall he is anyway he is sweet and we had such an amazing time. He showed me pictures of his daughter, she is three and just about the cutest thing ever. Apparently, his ex-wife is something of a crazy mess and he just couldn't take the verbal abuse any longer so he left. It makes me a little sad to think that anyone would treat him so poorly, he is simply the greatest!

Joshuwa and I have been on a few dates now and things have been going so well. I feel so comfortable with him and I love to get lost in his kisses and just be near him, so I thought I was ready to have alone time at his house. But when things started getting steamy, we were taking each other shirts off and everything was great until, his hand found its way into my pants. I freaked out, I jumped up threw my shirt and shoes on and ran out. I didn't think about how I was going to get home on foot from Garden Grove, but I couldn't go back. I acted so foolish, he was not hurting me, gosh being raped really screwed me up. As I was walking and thinking, Joshuwa found me and made me get in the car. He felt so bad, he kept telling how sorry he was. He said he would wait until I was ready. He was so worried that he had done something wrong or made me feel pressured; it hurt me to hear the words coming from his mouth. So, I had to explain everything to him, which at first felt so uncomfortable and dirty, I didn't want him to think I was just some dumb blonde, I didn't want him to look at me like I was some dirty bitch, some whore asking for it, like the cops did that night. But he didn't, in fact he held my hand and kissed it as shook recalling every detail of that night. As I spilled the truth and cried, he held my hand and cried with me. The only thing he had to say was how much it hurt him to hear that I went through any of it, that nobody should have ever hurt me or any woman like that. He said understood and that we could take things slow if I need to. He is just so amazing.

Joshuwa and I finally had sex, and it was amazing. He was so soft and tender with me and really made love to me. I don't think I have ever been more in love with anyone. He smells like a mixture of wax from his hair product and Lucky You cologne, I love to get lost in his smell. With his body on mine and feeling him inside me I just felt a love and happiness I have never known. The sexual pleasure of being with someone you love is so much deeper than I ever knew it could be. Joshuwa just makes me so happy and I love spending time with him, and I enjoy just hanging out watching Viva La Bam with him on the weekends. We also love going in the pool with his dogs. Joshuwa makes me feel so special, like I am the only woman in the world. He is always taking pictures of me or filming me and it makes me laugh. He told me I was too beautiful to not be in front of the camera.

Things have truly been wonderful between Joshuwa and I over this past year; he even came to stay with me at the Disneyland Hotel during my family vacation, that definitely made it extra special. He has been really feeling down lately though, I guess the custody battles over his daughter are taking a toll. Plus, he just got out of jail not that long ago, I wonder if that has impacted his case. He was in for a week because he beat up some creep that was harassing some woman, he saved her from being sexually assaulted in an alley behind a bar. The judge handling his case ruled in his favor, and cut him loose with time served. The thing is, now he keeps asking me what I would do if he died tomorrow. I don't know why he is asking me that and I don't know how I feel about him even asking me, let alone what I would do. I love him so much I don't know what I would do without him. He is so amazing and we never fight, we always have so much fun and he is really good to me.

Joshuwa got really upset with me yesterday when I asked him if he wanted to go see my friend's band play, because he found out we have a mutual friend, Ben. He really didn't like the idea of me going to Ben's shows without him or that I talk to Ben at all. Joshuwa said he didn't trust Ben and he didn't seem to be jealous. Which spiked my interest in the matter so I probed a bit deeper with questions as to why. Joshuwa told me that Ben just really is not a good guy, that he is creep that takes advantage of women. He said when Ben sees that a woman may be vulnerable or not thinking clearly, he swoops in to hit it and quit it. I never known Ben to be that way but I tucked that information in the back of my mind.

I met up with Ben tonight to talk about Joshuwa; I told him how Joshuwa didn't like us hanging out and Ben told me, Joshuwa had already told him as much. I told him I had a bad feeling, that Joshuwa was going to do something stupid and that he kept asking me what I would do if he died. It was just so strange that he kept asking me that question day after day, and I am sure he could see that it made me squirm. Ben told me maybe he was just going through some stuff with his daughter and baby mama, that he was just having some trouble working through it. Ben could be right but still I wasn't so sure. I was still really worried and I still had a gut feeling something bad was going to happen.

I went out with Joshuwa tonight, I missed his call to sit with him while he got a new tattoo, so we met up at his place after. We went and picked up one of his friends and I drove them to a bar to have some drinks and play pool. We had so much fun the guys were getting really goofy and just enjoying the night out. Joshuwa looked so handsome in his white button-down shirt, his black Dickies and black and white Chuck Taylors. I couldn't stop looking at him. After we dropped his friend back at his house we were heading back to my car, and he grabbed me, spun me around and kissed me. I laughed and asked him what that was all about, he said "I just wanted to kiss the sexy woman I am so in love with." Then we got in the car and I took him through the drive thru at Del Taco. He was a little drunk so ordering was a bit funny. He wanted a red burrito with no red sauce! The cashier was trying to ask him if he just wanted the bean and cheese burrito, and was getting frustrated. So, I just asked her to place the order as he asked. It was really funny. He was eating in the car and got some sauce on my glove box. It was no big deal I can clean it up later. When we got back to his house, we made love and fell asleep. I left in the morning promising to meet him later for dinner and a movie. I was a little bummed that we missed the Lilo and Stitch movie in theaters, but it will be on DVD in a week. So, I will let him pick the movie. I am so confused and upset, I don't know what to think. I was getting ready to go meet Joshuwa for our date, I mean I had gotten through all my makeup and was curling my hair, when he called. He sounded like something was deeply wrong when he spoke. He told me that he had to cancel our plans because he needed to spend some time with his daughter. I told him ok, but asked if anything had happened and why he sounded so down. He told me it was tearing him up to have to decide between the two people he loved most in the world, on spending his time with. I told him he was being silly and that it was no big deal, we could go out another night. I understood that while he was fighting for his daughter, he had to go by his ex-wife's wishes and not let her meet me "the girlfriend." He then told me that he had to go far away for a long time and that he loved me and wanted me to be happy. When I asked him if I would see him again, he just told me that the next time I see him he wasn't sure if I would even remember him. I was full on crying at this point and I asked him if I could go with him. He told me I couldn't follow him where he was going, no one could. Then we told each other we loved each other and hung up the phone. I still have not absorbed the conversation.

CHAPTER 23

THE LOSS OF MY HEART

I was having the worst dream that I could not seem to wake from. It was about Joshuwa being dead in his room, but he was also next to me talking to me and crying with me holding my hand telling me he was sorry. I was struggling to open my eyes when my phone rang really early this morning. It was Ben, he told me I needed to sit down he told me that he had something important to tell me. I started crying before he even spoke another word. It was like somehow, I already knew it was bad news about Joshuwa. When I told him I was sitting, Ben told me that Joshuwa had shot himself; that his roommate found him dead on his bedroom floor this morning. I couldn't believe it was true, so I hung up on Ben and frantically tried calling Joshuwa and his ex-wife answered his phone. When I asked her where Joshuwa was, my heart sank as she told me so coldly, "Joshuwa is dead sweetie." I hung up, thinking it was some bad joke; it couldn't possibly be true.

I couldn't breathe and surely couldn't talk, so I grabbed my keys and told my mom in broken hyperventilating mumbles that I was leaving, and rushed out the door. As I got onto the 405 to get to Garden Grove as fast as I could, my mind was a complete mess and I couldn't tie down one single thought. The 22 was a bit more of a traffic jam which was strange it was usually the opposite way around, but I took the time to pray harder than ever before that this wasn't true. When I turned into his neighborhood, I really starting to feel sick as I followed his street around to his house. When I got there, they were just throwing his stuff in the trash like he didn't matter.

His roommate Dan came walking up to me as I got out of the car, as he was approaching me, he told me that Joshuwa was gone. I collapsed in the street, I felt like someone had just punched me in the chest and I couldn't feel my legs. I couldn't feel anything but the cracking of my heart, it was almost as if I could hear my heart breaking. How could Joshuwa do this to me, to himself or to his daughter? Paul had to carry me and put me in a chair on the lawn until I was able to somewhat gather myself. Once I was able to calm down a bit, I wanted to see his room, so Dan lead me to Joshuwa's room.

There was a huge chunk of carpet cut out and the wood flooring was stained in his blood. There was a chunk of wall cut out from where the bullet landed after he shot himself. I sank down into the hole in the carpet and cried. I could smell him, the smell of his cologne, his hair wax, his pineapple and cilantro candles and the metallic, salty heavy smell of his blood. I just wanted him to be here holding me, I wanted to feel him next to me, I just wanted to feel anything other than this horrible pain in my heart. After what seemed like hours, I started yelling at everyone to get out and stop touching his stuff. I told them to stop throwing away his belongings like he didn't matter. It was like they were all throwing him away, working to erase him completely. I could still smell his Lucky You cologne all over the room, and I got up and grabbed everything I could fit in my car. I was in so much pain and I was just trying to push the pain away, praying to wake up from this bad dream.

When I got home, I called Joshuwa's phone to find out when services were going to be, from his ex-wife. Because his dad had him cremated, they were having a wake for him. I asked Cathy where the surfer Build-A-Bear was that I had bought him and my other stuff that I had left there. She said she would bring the bear. Will was with me at the wake and it made it feel easier. Cathy kept making me feel super uncomfortable; and finding out that Joshuwa had a fifteen-year-old son from his high school sweet heart was even a little more hurtful. It was like Joshuwa felt he had to hide pieces of himself from me, but that was not true. I love him and always will, I would have never judged him or put conditions on my love. I got the bear back but my sandals Cathy was wearing and I am pretty sure my bras she kept too. What a crazy bitch. I just want to go home and die.

Everything seems to be covered in haze, it is as if I can't get through this. I keep calling Joshuwa's phone now that Cathy powered it off, just so I can hear his voice. I recorded his messages to me onto a tape so I wouldn't lose them, I need to hear his voice. I bought the Lilo and

Stitch 2 movie we were going to watch together. Boy was that a mistake and the new Mariah Carey song "We Belong Together" isn't helping either. There is a hole so deep in my chest I can feel it in my soul, it is like my heart has been ripped out and now there is just an open bleeding cavity where it used to be. Is this nightmare ever going to end? I just want to go back in time just so I can see his face one last time and beg him not to do this. I spend my nights praying to die and my mornings crying because I woke up. I can't remember the last time I went out; I just feel so broken, and I can't seem to gather my broken pieces to put myself back together again. I have been stashing Jack Daniels under my bed to help take the edge off. But drinking just makes me feel worse.

It has been a few months and keeping a journal of how I feel seems to really be helping. The nun at church suggested it, and she is right there is so much I have unsaid to Joshuwa and I just need to get it out, even if it is on paper. It has also helped getting out of the house with my new friend Jerry. He is so much fun to be around and he just got out of a long relationship so we can comfort each other with laughs. I never thought I would have fun again but Jerry is good company. Ben came over to see me but my mom made him stand in the street because he looks like the devil to her. It was so ridiculous and I was really embarrassed. I have been talking to this other really awesome guy that seems like he would make another great friend. He is going to do a tattoo for me, that I want to help me remember and still let go of Joshuwa. It will represent that the past is gone and behind me and my whole life is ahead of me. I can't let myself die with Joshuwa.

Well Joshuwa was so right about Ben! Ben has been trying to hang around me a lot and trying to get me alone. He actually acted like he was comforting me and then tried to kiss me. Then to add insult to injury he tried to coax me into sleeping with him. He tried to tell me that it would make me feel better if I just ripped that Band-Aid off and got it over with. What a jerk, I can't believe I didn't just listen to Joshuwa and stay away from Ben.

CHAPTER 24

ANDY

Wow, when I went into the tattoo shop to meet Andy, he was so much hotter than his photos. I really can't believe how comfortable I am around him either. After five full hours on the tattoo table, I am really liking Andy. He is so sweet and even tried to keep me covered while tattooing my hip, it was really sweet. And something about the way his hands seemed so gentle when he wiped up my tattoo it gave me chills. Things were so cool between us we are going to hang out this weekend when we both have some free time.

When I got to Andy's he was so excited to see me and his nervous smile made him look even more adorable than before. I gave him a huge hug and his arms were strong and he smelled like a familiar soap, but I couldn't place it, I just let the fragrance fill my nose. He invited me in and we spent all night talking and laughing, learning more about each other. It was past two o'clock in the morning when I was leaving; he walked me to my car. He even opened my car door for me, and then he asked to kiss me. It was the sweetest most tender kiss and I felt both happy and sad. Happy because I wondered what could be between Andy and I, and sad because I missed Joshuwa so much I almost felt guilty.

When I got home, I couldn't wait to call Jerry and tell him all about it, he has become my best friend. But I will have to wait until morning because it is just too late.

When I called Jerry, I told him everything about the night I had with Andy, he was so happy for me and glad to hear me so happy. I told him about the pang of guilt I felt over the kiss, and he made me feel better about it. Jerry reminded me that Joshuwa loved me and would want me to be happy and find new love. He also reassured me that it was ok to still love Joshuwa. We decided I would meet him out for drinks to celebrate my new-found happiness. Gosh Jerry was such an amazing friend.

I don't know why but Jerry drank more than he usually does and we ended up lip locked in a kiss, but nothing else happened. I think we both just had too much to drink and got swept up in all the fun and laughing. He slept in the bed next to me which was nice because it was kind of cold. I am so confused now, that kiss has me feeling like I have to figure out what I want and what is going on in my life. Why does my life always seem to be like a crazy train or a roller coaster? I just need to catch my breath and figure things out. I am seeing Andy tomorrow so maybe I will have a better idea about what I truly want, after that!

I went over to Andy's and we had a few drinks while we watched a movie. He showed me some of his art and it is amazing. He is really something special and his art is so good it should be in art galleries; some of it could really change the world. Change it in the way of making the world a more beautiful place and bring joy to the hearts of so many people who enjoy art. Some people really get deep about how a piece speaks to them on individual levels. He is so humble though and it is a bit refreshing. We went to his room to go sleep off the drinks we had, and we were kissing and caressing each other. Things were just hot and heavy; one thing lead to another and we ended up having sex. Don't get me wrong the sex was wild and fun, the thing is; I don't know where we stand. Sleeping with him just added confusion and more questions, what were we doing? Were we going to continue to see each other and see where this road takes us?

When I got home, I got ready for classes feeling a bit hungover and also happy. I really like Andy and I am excited to see what happens next in our journey and where it leads.

Classes were long today maybe because I couldn't shake this hangover, and I just wanted to sleep. When I got home, I called Andy he is working at the tattoo shop until late tonight, and since it is so close to thanksgiving, I figured I would bake him something. I made him a nice dessert and took it to him at the shop for him and his co-workers. He seemed so weird this time, like he didn't want to see me. I wonder what I did wrong. I will try not to think about it, maybe he is just having a rough night. When I got back home from dropping off the dessert, I got a text from Andy saying he wants to see me tomorrow.

I was so happy when I got to Andy's house, I never thought I would feel this happy again. It feels really good, and Andy makes me excited about life and the mystery of the future. We spent the night watching music videos and talking about music and life while we drank. Then we had sex all night long then I slept in his arms and left in the morning.

Over the past couple of weeks Andy and I have been seeing each other when we can. We have been having sex every time we see each other. Of course, I have been enticing him at times modeling my cutest bras and new lingerie. He seems to really enjoy looking at me and touching me and it really makes me feel sexy and desired. It's funny because I never thought that I would really like him as much as I do, or enjoy his company and his touch so much. My heart is exploding with excitement at the thought of him, he is really sexy and manly and really makes me laugh and smile. Just the thought of possibly having a future with him is exciting. Even though the thought that he never wants kids is kind of a scary thought for me when considering a future with him. I know that someday I want to get married and have children, I love the whole family unit and the fun and memories that can be made in a family. Oh well, I shouldn't over think it right now because I am just coasting along seeing where this leads.

My heart sank to my stomach when I got a text from Andy saying we needed to talk. So, I called him, he told me maybe I shouldn't tell someone everything about me next time. I didn't even tell him everything, there are secrets I am harboring that are locked up so tight I have never told another living soul. He told me that he didn't want to see me again. Whatever I don't have time for games I need to just focus on classes and forget about it. I am not surprised I mean what did I expect? To find forever with him? He got what he wanted I was just a fuck, a wet hold for him to get his dick wet then he tossed me aside like garbage. It is like I didn't even matter and the sting of it really hurts but I will get over it. I mean hey maybe I don't matter and maybe I just need to take the hard-learned lesson from this. It does not matter what show people put on in front of my face, it matters who they really are deep down inside, but nobody will ever take their masks off until they are ready to destroy you. Only those who don't give a hell what anyone thinks, or are too bold or too stupid to care, show their true colors all the time. I know one thing for absolute certain, I am not going to let another man hurt me! Men don't deserve that kind of power over me.

CHAPTER 25

MY BIGGEST MISTAKE

Jerry and I have been spending so much time together and we talk nonstop on the phone. He really is so handsome but I am afraid to lose him as a friend so I won't tell him about my growing feelings. How could I have been so blind. We have been friends for over a year now and I never noticed what was right in front of me. Jerry is smart, funny, successful, and sweet, he just really seems to have his shit together. "Come on Gwen get it together and bury those feelings you are going out tonight with Jerry and he can't find out, not now."

So, everything was going great with Jerry while we were hanging out at a bar in Sunset Beach playing pool. When we stepped outside to get some air, he pulled me into his arms and kissed me. His arms made me feel cocooned in safety, his lips were soft and gentle and he smelled so good. I wanted to let myself get lost in the magic of the moment and I did for a minute, but then fear hit me. In a moment of wondering what would happen if I lost his friendship and how far I might crumble, I snapped out of my love trance. I pulled back from kissing him and I asked what he was doing, then looked at me and he said he was falling in love with me. I wanted to tell him I love him too, but I just couldn't lose my best friend. So, I told him we are friends, I explained to him how I cherish him and his friendship and that my fear of losing him permanently, if things went a rye between us. Then......I threw up all over him. Yeah not my greatest or finest moment. Because Jerry is such an amazing man he didn't even get upset about it, and he drove me home and carried me into bed. The next day he brought my purse to me because he forgot to grab it, he gave me a big hug and kissed me on the forehead and told me he would call me later.

Jerry is really hurt and when I called or texted him, he wasn't responding, taking my calls or calling me back. Finally, after a two or so weeks of blowing me off he called me and told me he can't talk to me anymore, he said I really broke his heart. He told me looking at me, hearing my voice, any of it was just too hard for him to deal with. He said he couldn't just forget the fact that he is in love with me. I wish I could change the way I responded. I wish I could change my vote because now my heart is broken too. I never wanted to hurt him and really didn't want to lose his friendship, but it seems like that is exactly what happened. I hurt someone I really love deeply and cherish so much, I am such a horrible person.

CHAPTER 26

ROCKSTAR CORRUPTION

After everything that has happened over the past few years I just need to escape. So, I am going to call my friend Tammy and find out if she will go with me to West Hollywood, and hit up a bar with me on the Sunset Strip.

Tammy and I are on our way to the bar and I am so happy, "twenty-three is going to be a good year for me!" I told her. When we get to the bar, we pay the door cover and go in, it is so cool. I can't believe how many people are here and so many people are talking to me. The guys here seem really cool and more my type, I love the rocker look but I wonder if I am cut out for the life style. I am pretty strong now from all the things I have live through so this could be what I have been searching for. Something with a little adventure where I can keep my walls up, not fall in love and just have fun living life. Isn't that what the rock n' roll stars all do?

Tammy had to fill me in on the missing pieces of the night the next morning, I guess I drank a bit too much. I did laugh a little from embarrassment when she reminded me about passing a famous rock star on the stairs to the upstairs bar. Apparently, alcohol had me thinking it would be a good idea to lean over and tell him, "Hey, you're hot wanna come home with me?" Tammy had to tell him there was no way she was allowing it and she said he was ready and willing. I feel so embarrassed. I don't know what is worse the fact that I asked another human being so bluntly to have sex with me or the fact that I didn't recognize him because I was plastered. Next time I won't drink so much. It just seems like I needed to blow off steam with a girlfriend I could trust. I knew Tammy would be the perfect gal pal for the job, she is just one of two bitches that are my ride or die friends. I have told both of them everything, well almost everything about my life. It turns out their lives haven't been such a cake walk either, everybody has their own baggage.

The nights spent at the bar on Sunset were always so much fun and I have made so many cool new friends. Jan is always here and sits at the end of the bar with the rest of our group of friends. I love, love, love to walk through and mingle with a crowd. I have found that I really enjoy meeting new people and I am really good at making friends. I met this really cool guy, he is a professional musician, Corey, he is pretty fun to hang out with. I just don't know if I am into him because he is cool, his status or for the attention of his friends. His group of friends are pretty cool and he seems to like my friends as well. I never thought I would be so chill and laid back and just plain comfortable around men again. My walls are not coming down though, I need them to protect my heart or at least what is left of it......if there is any left at all.

Corey and I have been seeing each other for about a month and things are going well. I never thought I would have so much fun with anyone, ok but when I say that I really mean all of his friends. I am not terribly attracted to him, and I don't think I will ever be "in love" with him, but maybe I can grow to care about him. He has asked me to move in with him so I have given my notice at work and started packing some of my stuff. Mom seems to be really worried about my moving in with Corey but I am excited, I will finally be free. Not that my parents are super strict, I would just like to not have to explain myself or have twenty questions all the time. I know they are just asking because they care, but I still just want this stepping stone to being on my own. For now, we will live in his studio in Sherman Oaks. He doesn't like to tour anymore because he is forty-five and it is rough on your body being on tour, so he is working at a fly by night talent agency.

The first few months I was so bored until the evenings or the weekends, being cooped up in the studio apartment was more boring than I could take. But we are moving to a bigger place and I am painting and moving our stuff while he is at work. I love the new apartment it is so much bigger and we have more space. Our cats seem to be happier too, Scottie especially, I have had him since after Joshuwa died so he is really my rock and comforts me. I can't wait until we can get a new couch there wasn't room in the studio but I am ordering one today. I am so happy.

Corey came home today in a really bad mood and told me he didn't want to talk. I tried to find out what was wrong but he just ignored me and jumped on the computer. Maybe I need to start working and get out some, plus I will have my own money again since what I had saved, I spent on furniture for the apartment. After Corey left for work, I went on the computer to answer some friends on Myspace and Facebook and send out some resumes, only he left his email open. I wasn't going to read through it, but a subject line caught my eye, "Yes I want your cock." I opened it up and read it, it was a man he had been speaking to for weeks and arranging to meet him up for sex. I was so disgusted, he has been trying to meet up with men for sex behind my back. Message after message was men arranging to meet him in different places and hotels for sexual encounters. My head was swimming, why would he be with me if he is gay, who does that? I was so angry I just needed to get out of there. So, I grabbed my phone and my keys and went to walk it off and regroup.

As I am walking now down the street, I can't get the thoughts or images out of my head. These men talking about giving each other oral sex and then giving and / or taking cock. I have nothing against gay people or what they do or who they love, but this wasn't that. Corey has me tangled up in some kind of sick twisted life style while he has his cake and eats it too. I am relived now, that he doesn't really bother me for sex and that I always make my partners put condoms on no matter what. I need to call someone to come get me out of this twisted web of sex, lies and deceit. I didn't know who else to call so I call Trevor and tell him everything. Trevor and his new girlfriend come to my rescue thank goodness because I left my car with my mom so she could use it.

By the time Trevor and his girlfriend arrive I have taken the time to print and tape all the dirty messages all over the apartment, and have my things packed. Before we start loading up the car Trevor and his girlfriend start reading some of the messages. Trevor even finds one that leaves him so disgust he takes a photo of it with his phone to show the guys. As he is busy doing that, I am writing down the recipe for the dinner I had planned to cook that night. I open the fridge and leave it on top of the chicken then head into the living room to see if I missed anything. Then we load up all my stuff, then the cats and leave. I was at least kind enough to leave a note in the fridge detailing how to cook dinner for Corey, so he shouldn't be too upset that I left. After all the messages I read and printed, I just don't want to speak to him.

When I get home, the smell of the house is clean as usual and the scent of moms wax warmer is crisp in the air; I am where I should be. After unloading the car and Trevor's girlfriend helping me unpack, I am just so thankful to see my old room and bed. I shower off and then slip into my pajamas and climb into bed with my cats and go to sleep. The craziness of the morning and having to come home with urgency really wore me out. I was so mentally and emotionally drained, I just needed to shut my brain down for an hour or so. I was awakened a few hours later to my phone ringing, seriously; Corey is calling me. I ignore his calls and texts for the rest of the night and sleep off my anger. I am so sickened by his lies and betrayals I don't care what he has to say.

For a week Corey has been calling and texting, telling me it was some misunderstanding and how sorry he is. I am just not so sure I believe him or that I want to at this point. I mean what kind of fool does he take for? How do you accidently have hundreds of sexual conversations with other people and call that a misunderstanding? I read every word and I understood perfectly that he is in fact very sexually attracted men and he enjoys their sexual company. Then as if this week can't get any worse, I see a letter on the porch with my name on it. It is from Rob, I don't know why he won't go away and leave me alone. He has been stalking me for years and this is just getting old. I guess he thinks that telling me that he has been watching me will what impress me? It is just creepy and I think it is time for some kind of restraining order. I can't just try to ignore it and hope he goes away, it has been going onway too long now and he is still stalking me.

I am so frustrated I tried to get a restraining order on Rob, but it hasn't even gone through yet and as soon as he was served with papers to appear in court he flipped out. He followed me home from a night out with the girls and hit me with his car. I am so stupid for not being more aware of my surroundings. How could I have not noticed I was being followed. I have a huge bruise from my shoulder to my ankle that wraps around half of my body. I am so sore but even more so I am mad. I am just lucky my injuries are very minor and not more serious. The officer that came out to do the report, literally asked me what I wanted him to do about it. "Ummm...how about your job and arrest him!" You would think that you would not have to tell the cops how to do their job. Seriously, what else would you do with someone who committed attempted murder and assault with a deadly weapon, besides arrest them? I can't believe they are telling me there isn't anything they can do without a restraining order. So basically, if I don't have a fancy piece of paper to throw at my stalker in hope of distracting him so I can run away, the cops can't arrest him for the crime he committed. "Oh, Jesus Christ please help me, I need your help." It seems like I am floating in so surreal nightmare unable to wake up.

After my near-death experience of being run down by a car manned by my crazed stalker, I decided I would hear Corey out. Maybe it was just a misunderstanding, who am I to say? Maybe he was letting a friend use his email and computer, how do I know? I am not sure anymore. So, I am giving him a second chance and moving back in with him. This time though I will be working too, at the talent agency he is working at. I am going to work for their online talent gossip page and I am sure I will love it.

CHAPTER 27

SECOND CHANCES

I am really starting to regret giving Corey a second chance. The first couple of months back were fine and we were having so much fun. Working and then meeting up with our friends. He got me a nice bottle of Daisy perfume for Christmas, it isn't exactly my taste but I won't tell him that. At first using some coke here and there didn't seem so bad. I mean we were all partying and it seemed ok. It just made me strangely tired which is weird, and Corey kept yelling at me to get up. So, I don't dabble with coke anymore, I would rather not. Corey is just using obscene amounts of coke and I hate how moody he is.

When we got home from work Corey was in a mood, I told him I was going to shower and then cook dinner. He just ignored me and went about looking for his coke stash in the closet. When I was almost done in the shower, I felt this searing pain in my scalp, Corey was dragging me out of the shower screaming about some phone call. I had no idea what he was even talking about. He kept my hair held tight and started punching me hard in the face. The first blows were bone on bone pain and I could feel the heat and throb in my face. Then he smacked me across the face and I felt the flesh of my lip split open, I could taste the metallic flavor of the blood as my lip bled. While he was hitting me a kicking me, I was begging him to stop and trying to get the fingers of his hand he had wrapped in my hair loose. Finally, after trying to defend myself from all the blows, I had to try to fight back. I was wet, naked and cold and just wanted him to stop hitting me. He said Bill had called from the office, I didn't understand why that was such a big deal. There was probably an issue with one of the stories or a computer, but Corey was sure I was cheating. It baffled me why he would even think I was cheating or where he thought I would find the time. I worked all day, we went to work together and came home together and he never let me out of his sight. I told him he was just being paranoid, that only seemed to fuel his anger.

He was dragging me around the apartment by my hair, kicking me in the ribs and stomach. The blows to my face and head went almost unnoticed as my fear and adrenaline built up. All I could think about was how I needed to get free of him. After beating me for what seemed like an hour, he pushed me outside and locked the door. I was cold and naked, I couldn't believe it. I sat down trying to cover myself with my hands and legs. As I sat huddled with my knees brought to my chest and my heels pressed into my bottom to both cover myself and to keep me as warm as possible. I needed to calm down and focus on what to next to get back inside. I thanked the Lord for the fact that Corey had snorted so much, it meant he drank more. With his body plied with drugs and alcohol he stumbled around more and his blows weren't as hard as they could have been. I just put my head on my knees and let the tears stream down my face as I tried to ignore the pain in my ribs and my face. I was trying to forget the smell of alcohol on Corey and the coldness in his eyes while he beat me.

An hour later, when one of the neighbors got home from work, he gave me his jacket and pounded on the door until Corey opened it. When I got back inside, I thanked our neighbor and retreated to the room and locked the door. I was so thankful to get inside the warm apartment. My toes, fingers and lips were blue from the cold. I got dressed in the warmest clothes I could find and bundled under the blankets to get warm and cried myself to sleep.

The next morning as we drove to work Corey told me how sorry he was and that he loved me too much. He said he was just so afraid of losing me. He told me he just freaked out because I had left before without even telling him I was going. I didn't know how he wanted me to feel, think or respond, my lip was busted open, my cheek was swollen and my eye was black and nearly swollen shut. I had bruises all over my body and I couldn't hide them all. I was angry; angry that he beat me up and angry that I endured it. I was too ashamed to tell my parents, what would they think of me? I would be some little weak girl in their eyes if they found out, or at least that is how I felt. Work was an even bigger stress, with everyone asking me what happened and being so nice. I lied and told them that I had tripped and fallen down some stairs. It was so humiliating but I just didn't want people in my business.

I feel so lost and broken; I don't know how to change that, but being with Corey isn't what I want, not after he beat me up.

CHAPTER 28

MORE CARNAGE

A few days later I was healed up enough to take the car and sneak off to see my family. All evidence of abuse I had left was some very mild bruising under my eye which I covered with makeup, thank you for the heavy-duty Kat Von D tattoo cover concealer! I waited for Corey to lay on the couch where he normally fell asleep watching tv in the afternoons every weekend. I told him that I was going to go over and sit with Jan's kids while she went out for the day and he waved me out. It was the kind of wave you get that makes you feel like a fly someone is trying to scoot away from them.

It took two hours to get back to my parent's house in the bumper to bumper traffic on the 405 freeway. But I was relieved when I finally got there, I felt the comfort and safety of my family as I walked in the door. Mom was doing laundry and dad was cooking lunch for everyone. The smell of spices, meat and vegetable filled my nose and made me think about how hungry I was. I have been skipping meals lately because I have been saving every penny I can, not to mention when I can eat, I just seem to forget to.

Mom was so happy to see me, tears pooled in her eyes and she jumped up to hug me. Her embrace made me feel protected and the smell of her Light Blue perfume surround me. I just stood there hugging her back and crying. I told her I was just crying because I missed her so much and she seemed to understand and believe that. There was no way I could tell her that Corey was slowly isolating me from them. He forbade me to see my family without his permission or him being there with me. I think he was worried I would say something to them about all the beatings and fights.

My visit home was flying by so fast and I didn't want to leave. We were all having so much fun, talking and playing games like when I was a kid. I just really wished Will was here but he was away at school. I was so proud of him for getting a scholarship to go to a big university.

Before I knew it, it was past ten o'clock, and I started to panic. How could I have lost track of time like that? I checked my phone which I kept on silent during my visit, there were over one hundred and fifty missed calls and texts from Corey. My stomach immediately tied in knots with fear, he was demanding to know where I was and when I was coming home. He made threats about what was going to happen if he had to come find me. I had to get back to the apartment. I told mom and dad I was getting tired and should head back. As I hugged them both goodbye mom and I both started to cry, I am sure her reasons were far different than mine. Then I got in the car and headed back, with dread in my heart.

When I opened the door to the apartment, Corey was waiting for me. The look in his eye was rabid and I braced myself for what was going to happen. He raised his hand and backhanded me with all his might and it made me stumble back. I started to cry and explain that I was sorry, that Jan had come back a few hours later than she thought she would. He wasn't listening to me he didn't care to hear my excuses. When he grabbed my hair to throw me to the ground, I kicked him, and clawed his arms. He then let go and told me I better learn how to behave like a woman should. The way he said it I knew something far worse was coming.

When he took his belt off, I thought he was going to walk away and lay on the couch like he usually did when he was done beating me. I couldn't have been more wrong. He then started smacking me in the face with each blow I became even more dizzy. I felt the blood trickling down from my eyebrow and down my chin from my lip. At some point the beating and struggling to get away caused me to bite my tongue and the amount of blood in my mouth was thick and making me feel sick. Then he grabbed me by the hair again and dragged me over to the bed and then threw me on it. I was shaking and crying and praying for him to just go away.

Things were quiet for a minute and all I could hear was the sound of his breathing. Then he asked me where I had been all day and night, and warned me not to lie to him. I stuck to my story about sitting for Jan's kids but all that did was set him off again. He started talking to me so softly it almost made my skin crawl with fear that nearly paralyzed me. He told me that he knew I was lying, that I was out with some other guy. He told me that I had no right to give my pussy to anyone else because I never gave it to him like an obedient woman should and he was going to teach me a lesson. I had no idea what that meant until he hit me again and then ripped my shirt and bra off of me. I was fighting to get away as hard as I could, I couldn't get raped again and certainly not by someone I knew and lived with. I managed to get flipped on my stomach and was clawing at the sheets to pull myself away from him but he was stronger than I was; he yanked me back down the bed and punched me in the stomach. Then he yanked my shorts down my legs as I struggled to fight back and then ripped my panties off. Because they were only G-string type panties, I felt them tear into the inner side of my ass cheek and screamed. I was begging him to stop, telling him he didn't want to do this and pleading with him to calm down. My words were all falling on deaf ears and by now our neighbors were use to hearing all the fights and beatings so they were just ignoring my screams.

Once he had my panties off, I was completely naked, crying and bleeding and I was still squirming to get away. He was holding me down by the chest with his left arm, and he quickly got his pants undone and his penis out. When I realized this was going to happen and I wasn't able to overpower him my fear and the spinning of my head were nearly too much. Corey then just shoved himself in me as hard as he could, and my body went limp with defeat. And I just laid there and let him rape me while I looked at the wall and cried.

While he was on top of me, violently and roughly shoving himself into me, I tried to let myself detach from my body and the pain. I wondered what it was that went through a man's head that made him believe he had a right to violate me. What was it about me that made men think it was ok to not listen when I said no? Then I thought about how I couldn't report my boyfriend for raping me, who would believe that? I learned that even when a stranger violates you it is hard to get anyone to listen. That last thought made me feel real anger and rage, because I knew that nobody was willing to listen to any woman about rape and abuse, because sadly there were so many that lied about it. Then I felt the sick and evil thought creep into my mind about how they should trade places with me or any other woman who has actually been a victim, so they could learn a good lesson. I found myself thinking about the time Maryann lied and made a false report about a guy she liked raping her because he stopped having sex with her, and I was sickened by the recollection. Lucky for him he was able to prove her a liar with an alibi for the date and time in question. Then my mind raced to thinking how men like the one raping me now will never be held accountable for their crimes because of women like Maryann, and I wished he was raping her and not me. But then I thought about how he has never even met her, then I immediately felt guilty for the evil I was wishing on her.

CHAPTER 29

THE VENOMOUS SNAKE IN MY BED

I am so confused I don't know what to do, Corey told me he was sorry and that it would never happen again. Was he sorry for hitting me or raping me? I was to afraid asking would set him off again and took his insincere apology while keeping silent. So, for now I am going to stick it out. I have feelings for him…. of distain and disgust. I don't think I have any feelings of care for him in my heart at all, I am just not sure about anything anymore. Things have been pretty calm this past month. We went to Las Vegas because he was playing in a blackjack tournament. It was fun until he wanted to go get married, I told him I didn't want to get married. I am only going to be twenty-three in a few weeks. I can't even think about marriage right now my life is a mess; the thought of it just doesn't feel right. Even if I wanted to entertain the thought of marriage, he would be the last person in that fantasy. He was so mad he went up to our room with some bitch off the casino floor. I wish the Hilton would have comped us two rooms because I just don't want to be around him. I am not even mad about the other woman because I haven't been having sex with Corey anyway. I never really had sex with him because if I am being honest I have never been attracted to him. I don't think I have ever loved him. I was more concerned about his temper than who he was screwing.

I had no idea what time it was when I got to the room, but it had to be after one o'clock in the morning. When I got up to the room and walked in, the air was thick with the smell of sweat and sex. The whore of a woman he brought up here was gone but Corey was not, he was sitting on one of the queen beds in the room drinking. He started grilling me about where I had been but I just laughed and told him, "why does it matter? You are fucking other bitches anyway." Boy was that a mistake, I knew it as soon as the words fell from my mouth. He looked at me with such anger and lunged at me with evil in eyes. I tried to run to the bathroom to get to safety but I lost my footing and he caught me by the arm. He yanked me back so hard I thought he would dislocate my shoulder and I felt a pain shoot from my shoulder to my elbow as I was jerked closer to him. He then backhanded me, the blow to my face stung so bad, I was shaking by the rapid succession of blows that followed. The punches just kept landing all over my face and body. I begged him to stop hitting me but he reeked of alcohol and I knew he was on coke too. There was no pleading with him, when he is this far gone on cocaine and liquor. He didn't even feel anything but rage and hate, it was like he morphed into another person entirely. The beating only stopped when we heard knocking on the door, it was hotel security making sure everything was ok. Of course, he lied and said everything was fine.

Corey left after the security guard left, so I laid there on the floor by the sink crying for a few minutes waiting for the room to stop spinning. He promised he would never hit me again and yet here I am beaten again. I crawled to the bathroom and took a long hot shower. As I sat at the bottom of the bath tub, I thought about how my life seemed to be spinning out of control. I kept thinking about all the crazy things I have survived, but I also felt like I was never in control of my life. When I saw the razor on the side of the tub I thought maybe if I could just end it all, but I turned my head away. I prayed for help... for another way. How could this be my life now? After the shower I called housekeeping to change the bedding. Then I went to the ice machine to get ice for my eye and face. After I filled a hand towel with ice, I climbed into bed holding the ice to my injuries. I just needed sleep, then I would be able to think clearly.

The next morning, I was so worried about the five-hour ride back home with Corey. I put sunglasses on to walk through the hotel to the car, I could feel everyone staring at me and I couldn't walk fast enough. Once we got to the car, I quickly threw my bag in the back and stayed quiet. Corey kept trying to make conversation with me, as if I would talk to him. When he started professing his love and adoration of me, I started crying, not because I was sad but because it was all bullshit. I hated him but I felt stuck now, the shame I felt thinking about what other people would think of me. Now more than ever I thought about what people would say because Corey told me it was my fault, he had to hit me. He said I was out of line and had no right to speak so disrespectfully to him, or not give him sex like women are expected to when they are in a relationship. He said I had my nerve after making him look like a fool declining to marry him, to even think that he had any other option. I am not sure who is at fault anymore all I know is I am very unhappy.

My friend Jan and Corey's friend Jason came by to watch the Superbowl. I thought we would have a good night, since the Steelers won. "Well think again Gwen!" Apparently, he didn't like how I was looking at Jason. Sure, Jason is a trillion times better looking, but I have enough on my plate with Corey's ups and downs, I don't need added trouble. This fight really takes the cake, he beat me until I just laid there and took the blows. I didn't have the fight in me to fight back anymore. I just wanted him to storm out and leave me alone. My soul is broken and I can't seem to find a way to fix it. How am I ever going to get rid of him?

CHAPTER 30

DEAD WEIGHT

I have tried to ignore the fact that Corey has decided he doesn't want to work anymore. The drugs and drinking seem to be all he wants to do. I didn't care too much at first because he would be passed out before I got home from work, or he would just be gone… out partying somewhere. But we need to make rent and he has spent everything on his irresponsible habits.

When Corey got home, I was sitting in the dark on the couch. When he came in, he couldn't see me and was fumbling around so I knew he was wasted. It made me feel a bit more confident knowing that he was that wasted; if he decided to hit me, the blows wouldn't be so strong and would not hurt so bad. I couldn't wait to have this conversation anyway, I was done. So, I asked when he planned to get back to working so we could pay the bills, he just snapped back and told me to get another job. I was so angry, I told him he was nothing more than a washed up has been. I told him he needed to stop living in the past, that he chose not to tour anymore; or was it that none of the bands wanted him? That was the moment I knew I had really done it. He ran at me grabbing me by the hair and yanking me down to the ground. He was kicking me and dragging outside, real fear was setting in, what was he doing? Then he bent down and told me to stand up, he pulled me into a hug and then shoved me as hard as he could. If the neighbor hadn't come out to see what was going on and been there to catch me by my waist I would have flipped over the railing. I was shaking with fear as Corey yelled and pushed the neighbor out of the way. Corey grabbed me by the arm and whipped me back into the apartment. I ran through the apartment and into the room locking it behind me. Then I ran to the bathroom and slammed the door locking it too. I was still in shock and was still processing just how far I had spiraled. My life was taking on a new shape of constant abuse and horror and the times I spent happy and smiling were becoming fewer and fewer. I wasn't entirely sure, but I was certain that I didn't like my life. Slowly I was becoming numb; a callus was growing over me so thick I couldn't deny it and my heart was beginning die and turn black, I could feel it.

After about an hour everything was quiet so I came out to see what was going on. Corey was sitting at the table with some coffee, he asked me to sit down so we could talk. He said he was sorry yet again, that he didn't mean to get so upset. I was so sick of the lies and the abuse, I was done watching him drink and snort his way through every penny he got his hands on. I was pissed that he took my checks and deposited them in his account, the frustration was just more than I could take or ignore. I told him I wanted him to move out and he said he would. Then he handed me a cup of coffee. We agreed things were just not going to work out between us and since he wasn't working and couldn't afford the rent, it would be best for him to move. I told him I was sorry about the way things turned out and about how toxic things were between us. He seemed to agree with that and we just sat quietly sipping coffee. There was a really bitter taste to the coffee, I really hated it when he put too much coffee in the filter, so I asked him how many teaspoons of coffee he used. He just chuckled and apologized and we went back to drinking our coffee in silence.

I don't remember anything after drinking the coffee. I mean it was pretty common for me to sleep like a rock after a pot of coffee because it didn't work for me like it did for everyone else. The thing that scared me was that I couldn't remember anything at all, similar to the experience you get when you drink way too much alcohol and blackout. So, when I woke up this morning in the hospital with a huge headache, I was terrified about what might have happened. Not being able to remember was very terrifying.

Jan is here, so I ask her what is going on. She told me that when I didn't show up to work, she came to check on me but couldn't wake me. She told me my breathing was so shallow she got worried and called 911, then she held a mirror from her purse under my nose to see if I was breathing at all. When I ask her how long I have been out she tells me two days. I can't believe it… two days!!! I guess Corey is claiming that I took some ibuprofen because I wasn't feeling well and was complaining about a headache, but accidently grabbed his bottle of Paxil in the dark. Yeah, that couldn't be further from the truth! I keep a bottle of ibuprofen in my purse and one above the fridge with the other cold medications, and he keeps his Paxil in the medicine mirror in the bathroom. He totally drugged my coffee to try to kill me and lied about. Now I really have to be careful. I need to get away from him.

When I come home from the hospital, I see Corey, he hugs me and tells me how worried he has been. His words are just more lies and bullshit, and I tune him out. He didn't even have the human decency to visit me in the hospital in the six days I was there. Considering he is the one that put me there you would have thought he would have at least shown up to avoid suspicion. Then Corey tells me he has a surprise for me, a plan about how we can make money. Which is big of him to even bring up considering he is the reason I was let go at work. Lucky for me they gave me a generous bonus so I wouldn't talk about what a scam their pseudo talent agency is. I am too tired to fight about the truth of what has transpired; so I just sit to listen to his cocaine filled idea. He hands me a bag with some of my club minis, G-string panties and bras. I have no idea what he is up to so I just get in the car. When he pulls into the parking lot of a strip club, I think… he is joking. He told me he was very serious and started threatening me to get out of the car. I was too afraid to fight back this time so I went into the club.

When I opened the door and stepped into the strip club the music blared in my ears so loud, I had to shout to the guard to ask to speak to the manager. As he led me to the manager's office through the club, the stale smell of the cigarette smoke in the air mixed with the pungent smell of alcohol and sweat filled my nose. The air and energy in the room was thick with impure intentions and desires, it sent a shiver down my spine. During my stage dances I was so nervous because I had no idea what I was supposed to do. The manager didn't tell me what I should do and the girls were no help, they just kind of throw you to the sharks. But the guys sure did seem to love me because I made so much money in two hours. Six hundred dollars later I was out the door and a little less stressed. But it was short lived because Corey took my money as soon as I got in the car.

CHAPTER 31

JOURNAL ENTRY

When I got back to the apartment, I was so shaken by everything that just happened I ripped open my dresser drawer and grabbed the pink journal Tammy gave me for my Birthday, and now here I am penning my thoughts.

I am still shaking so much from all the adrenaline pumping through me that even my writing is sloppy. I am trying to calm down but I can't seem to focus on anything except for what just went down. I never thought I would ever be "that girl," you know the one that gets naked for money. The titty bar was really overwhelming, the rules are pretty simple though. I could be anywhere on the stage until I expose my breasts, then I had to stay behind the tape on the stage. It was to keep the girls safe, I guess. I just wore a mini club dress with a thong and bra under it. Oh yeah you have to be sure that all your vagina is covered and when you bend over your asshole is covered. I sat backstage and watched three girls go on before me, trying to get a clue what to do.

Before I even put my foot on the stage I was sweating and shaking from stage fright. The club was so packed every seat was filled. I was really wishing I had taken a shot before I went on, but I was so nervous I was afraid I would throw up. I walked out onto the stage when my song started and the guys went crazy. As soon as I started dancing, trying to mimic the moves of the girls before me; I was finally able to just relax into it. I didn't know any pole tricks but I used it and the floor to be as sexy as possible.

I was so nervous to take my bra off as I was stripping, so I just closed my eyes and thought about Andy and how I used to love to dance and model my bras before taking them off for him. I just imagined that he was the only one in the club and as I did, I felt myself become comfortable. By the time my bra came off I was smiling and money was raining down on the stage. The yelling, cheering and whistling of the crowd made me feel empowered. I felt a power in being desired by a room full of men that couldn't touch me, that I would never speak to in public.

What is happening to me? The only thing I am upset about or uncomfortable with is the fact that Corey took my money; is this the beginning of the new person I am becoming? Where is the little girl that used to look forward to mommy hugs and curling up with daddy and Will for a movie? Do I even know her, was she real, where did she go?

The stress it is really getting to me lately and because I needed a job. The stripping gig is just not going to work for me. I didn't really like the girls. I am going to have to find something else. I need a real job and I need it fast so I can pay these bills!

CHAPTER 32

CUTTING FOR CONTROL

After the first night at the strip club I couldn't walk. I woke up feeling like I got hit by a big rig. So, I had to spend the next two days soaking in lavender Epsom salts. I don't know where Corey has been and frankly, I don't care. I am just thankful he is not here bothering me and being a jerk. Maybe I can finally just relax and he will stay gone.

My wishful thinking was short lived, Corey came in and seemed to be really wasted, which meant I needed to just stay out of his way. He came in the room and started pawing at me and trying to kiss me, and I thought I might vomit. The feeling of him touching me and on top of me was making me sick. So, I told him, "Please stop Corey, I don't want to have sex." He told me, "Come on babe I love you and it has been over two months." I got so upset that he really thought I would want him anywhere near me. I tell him, "it's not going to happen." He just looked at me with the look he gets when he is going to hit me. His eyes glazed over like glass with no depth to his soul. Because I was all too aware of what was going to come next, I flinched back putting my arms up in defense. I couldn't escape his blows and I knew it. He punched me in the eye and then the cheek. I tried to move away, but I just couldn't get away from him. He pulled me back and threw me down, grabbing me around my throat. I clawed at him trying to get him off of me, but he just moved out of my grasp. He squeezed tighter and tighter and I was desperate for air, I could feel my life fading from me. I thought, "This was it, this is how I am going to die."

I could hear knocking, someone is at the door! Thank you, dear lord. Corey climbs off of me to go get the door and I gasp and choke on the air I am gulping to fill my lungs with. I lay on the floor in the room crying, listening to the voices on the other side. It sounds like my friend from the talent agency Angie. She must have come by to drop off my last check. I am so glad she stopped by because there is no telling what would have happened. I heard Angie ask where I was but Corey just lied to her and told her I was at a job interview.

After Angie left Corey came back into the room and said, "Bitch, are you done acting up yet? Are you ready to fuck me or not?" I thought it better to just agree and let him do what he wanted. So, I nodded and kept my head down as I got up and followed him to the bed and laid down. When he climbed up on top of me, I just laid there and cried while he had his way with me. The feeling of the weight of his body on mine was crushing, and feeling his skin on mine made me have to fight back the vomit rising in my throat. He was so drunk he was rough and clumsy and he reeked; the smell of the liquor on his breath was thick and sickening. I hated feeling him inside me it made me feel violated and empty and I could feel the ice forming on my heart. I thought it would never end because he was still so drunk and high, he was having a hard time getting off. I just wanted him to cum and get the heck off of me. The longer it was taking the deeper into my mind I went. It was as if this was a new way to cocoon myself from the abuse. I just let my mind and soul float away while my body was being used for his sick pleasures.

When he was finished and rolled off of me to pass out, I got up to go to the bathroom to shower. I felt so dirty and unclean all I could think about was getting cleaned up. The sick bastard didn't even bother to take the dirty condom off, and I had no intention of helping him or waking him to do it, I just need to scrub him off of me. As I scrubbed away all the filth, I imagined shrinking small enough to flow down the drain and away from this life, I seemed to have been unlucky enough to stumble into. I could feel a new wave of nausea start to rise up my throat, and I scrambled out of the shower expelling every last drop of remains from my stomach. Once the waves of nausea stopped, I got back into the shower while I became broken down to tears. I am not the woman I thought I would be, I am crashing out of control on uncharted waters. My life has become as turbulent and as unforgiving as the sea waves crashing into rocks and cliffs. There was no control or sanity in my life and it seemed like a never-ending roller coaster of doom. I sank to the bottom of the shower and laid crying in the fetal position with my legs held tightly to my chest, wondering how to get control back in my life, or if I ever really had any control in my life at all. Then I saw my razor, I grabbed it digging the blade into my arm. It was not sharp enough to cut as deep as I hoped but it did cut me, and I felt a rush of euphoria explode in me. Cutting myself let my mind know I was in control. Only I could say how deep or how many cuts I put in my skin and if I wanted to go deep enough to end my life at that moment only I could say what happened; I felt a rush of knowing that nobody else had that much control over me. This new-found desire to cut myself took over and I used the razor to slice my skin open again and again pressing harder each time. By the time I had cut myself seven times and blood was running freely down my arm I threw the razor down. It was only then that I thought about hiding this, I didn't want to answer questions or explain myself to people who didn't really care.

After a good night's sleep on the couch I awoke feeling a new-found charge in my life and nobody could take it from me. When I went out later that night to the bar on the strip with my best friend Tammy, I was hyper aware. I looked around the group that I was standing in and could easily see all the pseudo friends within my circle, but suddenly I didn't care. It was as if once the wolves were exposed, I felt safer knowing I wasn't a lamb anymore, I was becoming a wolf. I had to change and morph into something stronger, though maybe I should take on a lioness and prowl these packs of wolves until I find my king. I took those thought and put them in a safe box at the back of my mind and thanked God for letting me see the truth.

While Tammy and I were dancing and talking to our friends, some woman, "Lisa" was her name maybe. Oh, what does it matter walks up to us and she tells Tammy, that she has been sleeping with her boyfriend? I couldn't believe it, Tammy would never do that and plus she has been seeing this really interesting guy that she met at the bar; which is now dawning on me that maybe that is where Lisa met him too because that is where we are. So, Tammy and Lisa walk off to start talking in the bathroom and I follow and just walk in to make sure things are ok with Tammy, she is really upset. Then when Lisa tells her she is going to be sick and runs into a stall. I felt all charged up from all my new-found self-power and kick the door in and pull her head back away from the toilet by her hair and ask what she means by that. When she says that she is just so sick he was playing them both, I calm down and say, "oh, well then…..as you were!" And then I shove her head back into the toilet and walk away. I grabbed another drink and then Tammy and Lisa wanted to go confront Danny. I was so ready to hear his excuses, but then when we got there, I had to pee so bad. This douche bag of a guy was just going on and on making excuses and playing games. So, I did what any other bestie would do, I grabbed an empty Gatorade bottle from the recycle can and Lisa's bestie then found some bushes. I had the other girl hold up her jacket to cover me while I peed in the bottle. When I was done, I dumped that bottle of pee all over inside and out of Danny's car. And we all left laughing. I felt wild and empowered. It felt good taking some kind of power back, even if it was only in my bestie's life and not really mine.

CHAPTER 33

VENTURING DEEPER INTO THE ABYSS

After feeling so powerful and strong like I was taking my life back, I decided I was going to just dive into the crazy. I was going to work at the peep show club in North Hollywood. I think it may be a bit calmer than the titty club I danced at a few nights ago. I just needed some real stripper gear so I grabbed some cash from Corey's wallet and head to Hollywood Boulevard to shop.

When I walked into the peep show club, it was darker than the other strip club, and it was lit with black lights. The carpeting was black with cartoon depictions of a beaver wearing a top hat, a girl's face, the silhouettes of dancers in different positions with and without out poles and martini glasses. It was also speckled with the illusion of confetti and everything was a mix of neon yellow, green, blue, orange and pink. The walls must have been an off-white color because only the door jams and the doors of the dancer's booths were glowing in the lighting; with window decals that said showgirls across the bottom and privacy blinds on the inside of the doors. The air smelled like bleach, sweat and cheap perfume. The energy was heavy and thick with shame, desire and bad intentions. When I made it through the beads to the store front, I asked for the manager. When the club manager, Miguel made it down the stairs he smiled and I told him I was looking for a job as a dancer, he led me to his office upstairs to fill out the paper work.

Right after choosing my stage name and my hours for the week I started work. I was so nervous I mean the peep shows are fully nude so that was a little bit intimidating. Being fully nude it also means the customers can't be intoxicated here. The little comfort I had was that the stage and the lap dances were topless only, meaning when I was completely nude, I was behind two thick pieces of glass separated buy a curtain. They just really throw you out to the dogs though.

My first peep show customer is a construction worker, I can tell because he is still in all his work clothes. He comes to me and asks for a peep show, I touch my key to the key reader and the curtain opens, after he pays. Wow, I have never seen someone undress so fast in my life. (Oh, we aren't supposed to tell them we can see them, it's a safety thing for us to be able to, but the tinted glass makes them think we can't.) "Man, this guy is really attractive and has some serious abs, he looks like he just walked off a Calvin Clein underwear photo shoot. "Ok focus Gwen, you need to start slowly dancing and stripping. Oh, wow this guy is so hard and he is starting to jerk himself off while watching me." I let all my thoughts flow through my mind freely as I strip down and put on a seductive display for the customer. Seven minutes goes buy so fast when you are feeling so empowered and desired, and he is feeding the machine more and more money. Every time the curtain starts to drop, he inserts the money he is holding in his free hand into the machine. He finally gets himself off while watching me and then leaves me a one-hundred-and-fifty-dollar tip. I do the math in my head and realize I just made two hundred and fifty-four dollars in a little less than an hour. I feel so pumped up on the feeling of being sexy and desired, I know I can make this work.

After my first peep show one of the other girls "Persway" comes over to the bench right outside my booth and starts talking to me. She is really friendly and really funny but also helpful. She tells me not to go topless on stage only in lap dances and to always take a lap dance to get a peep show. She gave me all kinds of tips and tricks to hustle money and it was really cool of her. She also told me the rules and illusion tricks to still look sexy or create a fantasy for the customers without breaking the rules. She tells me how to use the heel of my hand and finger tips to cup my nipples without ever touching them, and how to slap or place my hand close enough to the top of my vagina without ever touching it. Then she demonstrated a lap dance on me and starting teaching me floor and pole tricks on the stage. It was all so nice of her to give me so much information. I really think we are going to be great friends.

My next customer was not such a cake walk, and not for any other reason than my own silly brain. I took all my sexy clothes off and was standing just the way he requested me to. Then he picked up the phone receiver and tipped me so I picked mine up, and I asked him if he liked what he saw and all the sexy fantasy building talk. That is when he asked me to call him and dirty nigger. I was instantly flush red head to toe with embarrassment. I turned away and told him in my most innocently girly voice, **"I don't even think that's legal!"** Here I am standing stark naked in a peep show booth telling him I can't say that. He laughed and tipped me and so I said it for him. It was a bumpy show but I got through it. After that I knew I really had to step it up, it was my job to create a fantasy for these men and that is what I planned to do.

Most of the other girls were really catty and I just tried to stay clear of them. I did make a few friends though and it made the days and nights fly by so much faster. I worked a lot of double shifts to be away from Corey, I really hated him. I was always excited to start a new shift because it was the longest possible time I had before I had to see that miserable asshole again. I don't understand why he just won't get out of my apartment.

When I got home from work after every shift Corey expected me to give him the money, I had earned dancing. There was no way for him to prove or know how much I had made since boyfriends weren't allowed at the club and I was an independent contractor; so, I just handed him a couple hundred dollars and hid the rest. There was a loose board behind my books in the built-in wall shelves, that is where I hid my money. I needed to save enough to get away from him and not go running back to mom and dad.

I don't know what it is but something in me was starting to change. Maybe it was the feeling that with every day that passed I was that much closer to my dream of freedom.

CHAPTER 34

JOURNAL ENTRY

I am so glad that I have been writing every day and that Tammy gave me this journal. I never knew how important it would become to me or how much I needed to get everything out. I have been dancing for a few weeks now and I am making so much money, but I need to save a nest egg to get free from Corey and not have to ask my parents for help.

My parents know I am dancing now and they weren't happy about it, but they also didn't judge me which was nice. I had to sneak and call mom to ask her to take me to the doctor's appointment I have scheduled tomorrow. I had to give her the club address and explain to her that I had to work before I went to the doctor. Really, I just lied to Corey and told him I was working but I didn't put myself on the schedule for the day. Mom was really concerned about why I needed her to drive me, I told her Corey needed the car for some job interviews. I felt horrible lying to her but I couldn't very well tell her how abusive Corey is, or that he was aware of my ear infection but won't allow me to see a doctor. I have had this infection in my ear for a month and the over the counter drops are not helping. Corey doesn't care two shits how much pain I am in as long as I am making money every single day. I couldn't tell her any of it.

I have a few regulars that I have been making serious money from. They bring me new panties and socks with the tags still on or buy them in the store front and give them to me to wear on my shift. Depending on how long they want me to wear them depends on how much I charge them to get them back. I charge them three hundred an hour, so around four hours or half a shift to be more specific, is twelve hundred dollars. It gives me the freedom to go out shopping for more gear for work and also some things that I want, while still being able to save money.

I really must admit though, that although the money and being desired is addictive I really don't care for the life of stripping. It has changed my perspective on men and I have lost any hope that there are any good men left out there. The men flow in every night and look at me like a wild animal starving and on the hunt to quench their hunger. They prowl around the club under the illusion of darkness and shadows hunting and licking their chops, eyeing me from the corner of their eyes. I see them become hypnotized with the movements of my dancing body on the stage, sizing me up as a potential target for their release. Taking them through their illusions and fantasies step by step and hustling them out of as much money as possible. Their carnal desires draining their wallets and bank accounts, while they try to reach release. Lost in the fantasy of fucking me, they feed me money while jerking off on the other side of the glass. They act like animals sniffing the air wanting and hoping to catch the smell of pussy in the air, but never finding it. It is bullshit, it is all lie, a sick little game of cat and mouse, only I am the cat the hunter, the lioness on the prowl and they are my prey. I seek them out based on the level of desperation, perversion and desire they have. They all reek of it and I slaughter every one of them draining them, of the funds they need to pay their bills. So, I can't figure out which one us enjoys the game more or which one of us is the lesser of two evils.

Well I better go wash the filth of the of the days work off of my flesh.

CHAPTER 35

ALL IN A NIGHTS WORK

It has been a few months and I have seen such an array of people coming into the club. With the street entrance being a store front and the club being in the back through the beaded curtains, it is always fun to walk around and try to pull customers off the store floor for a dance when it is slow. There is a man that cross dresses and loves to come into the store and talk. He wears the most awful outfits. He is around four hundred pounds but he is tall so it only seems he is slightly overweight. He is always squeezed into crop tops and mini skirts that are far too small. The other day he was bent over the counter and I could see all of what God gave him, it wasn't a pretty sight. Then his makeup, oh don't get me started! I am in awe of good drag makeup any day, but this guy makes the world of drag a laughing stock. He doesn't even seem like he is trying, his eye shadow looks like he walked out of an 80's catalog with stripes of rainbow. His eyeliner and mascara are always smeared all over his eyes and his blush consists of just two bright pink, orange, or red circles. I am glad on days he isn't wearing lipstick because it is always all over his mouth and teeth and it is not pretty. He makes it harder to get the attention of anyone in the store, and I am not quite sure if it is because I can't stop staring or the customers can't. Tonight, was a real shit show though, when he asked to speak to the manager about getting a job as a dancer, I knew it wasn't going to end well. The store clerk called Miguel down to talk to the poor hopeful guy. When he was told he wasn't what the club was looking for, he started throwing stuff all over and the cops had to come escort him off the property. I felt kind of bad for him, who knows … he could have had fans. Now that I think of it maybe he does not even identify as a man maybe he identifies as a woman, which makes the whole situation a little sad and insulting for him or her.

It has been a long week working doubles, and aside from my regulars I have had some really interesting chaps come through. Persway and I always try to guess what they are like, and what they are into, what they might do for a living, before they come back through for their dances. So, while we were practicing some stage and pole work, we noticed an older gentleman, perhaps around 70 walk in. There was no way we thought he was there to get a lap dance or peep show. He looked long retired and like he should be at home with his little dog surrounded by photos of his grandkids watching television with his wife. So, imagine my shock when he requested me to give him a peep show.

Once I shut and locked my booth door, I touch

my key to the key reader to raise the curtain for the peep show, I had no idea what to expect. He was sitting in the chair with his pants down and as took the straps of my mini dress down I thought he was going to have a heart attack. He leaned forward in such a way that worried me but I had to continue on as if I couldn't see him. Then I seductively untied my bikini like dancer bra and I could see how big and excited his eyes got. Then I brought the lower half of my mini dress up facing away from him, leaving it around the smallest curve of my waist. With my full ass exposed in a thin red G-string I bent forward, slowly pulling it off and stepping out it. I heard a thud on the glass and saw him from between my legs touching it right at the level of my ass. So. I slowly backed into the glass and pressed my ass against it and pulled the skin at my hips to open up for him. I knew what this guy wanted. And the more I pleased the more money fell through my tip slot on the floor. I then stood up with my body still pressed to the glass and turned slowly around leaving my triple D cup breasts mashed to the glass in front of him. I was standing face to face with him and only I knew I could see him, I only reacted or responded like a trained seal when more money passed into my tip slot. As his tips fell to the floor, I ran my hands up the sides of my body and the pushed the sides of my tits together while I left a lipstick kiss on the glass at his lip level. When he dropped the fifty in my booth, I knew he was holding out his twenties for follow up peep shows and I sat back on the hip level dancing platform and kicked the button that drops the curtain. He rang my phone receiver and told me he had to get more money from the atm, so I waited with my key on the reader. When my curtain went back up, he was sitting with his hand stroking his penis. So, I got back on the platform and sat in a slightly c shaped curve at the hips with my back on the mirror behind me, he was tipping me and got close to the glass. When he was right at the glass and eyes wide, mouth wide open, almost drooling; I lifted my stilettoed feet and placed them close to my ass keeping my knees open. I was using the backs of my ankles to pull the skin on my ass apart opening my vagina because this guy was dropping fifties in my tip slot. Then I slapped the top front part of my pelvic bone just above my vagina and he dropped me seventy. He had me positioning and twerking and laying naked in that booth for over two hours before he finally kept at a steady pace of jerking his penis to get off. Which let's face it, that is what all these men intended to do in this club. I was so afraid that he wasn't going to make it out of that booth, I was sure several times he was going to have a heart attack. I couldn't wait to be dressed and out of my side of the booth just to be sure he made it. When he emerged ten minutes later, I was already on my way to do a lap dance for another customer. I smiled and gave him a wink because I took him for three thousand dollars.

Then there was the man who brought a shot glass in with him. He bought a few lap dances and then wanted a peep show. When he started jerking himself off, he grabbed the shot glass he had been carrying around and came in it. Then he picked up the phone and told me if I could get him to drink his own cum, he would tip me five hundred dollars. So, I started telling him how sexy it would be, how turned on I was just imagining him drinking his own cum and how much I wished I could see him do it; even though it was the most repulsive thing I had ever imagined and I could completely see him. Finally, after an entire excruciating minute of convincing he did it, he drank it down and then licked the glass clean. It was so disgusting I could feel chunks start rising in my throat but I had to choke it back. I acted real casual and leaned back onto the button to drop the curtain before time was up while still talking to him. Then I said sorry the peep show is finished and hung up. I needed to let the waves of sickness out and had to get to the restroom quick. Just when you think you have thick skin and you have seen it all, a little creeper pops out and makes proves you wrong. After throwing up a few times and washing my mouth out, I popped a piece of gum and walked back to the club and thought, "that guy really taught me not to be over confident and cocky, ok let's not go overboard he taught me not to assume I have seen it all!" I chuckled and got on with my night.

CHAPTER 36

JOURNAL ENTRY

Work has been really crazy and really busy. Tonight, there was a pimp that came in with two of his own girls trying to recruit the dancers. But security was quick to run them off the property. Now when I say pimp, I mean the stereotypical tacky suit and hat with a feather in it, walking with a rhinestone cane that he didn't need. He had a grill and was wearing more jewelry than ten people needed to accessorize themselves. I thought that was only on television and in some dumb adult cartoons. I really am seeing and learning new things every day.

Then later on Persway was talking to me about a hip-hop super star, we won't mention names here (just in case someone finds and reads my private journal.) Anyway, we are talking and I am sure she likes him and I tell her stop denying it and she is laughing. Then as I am telling her how it would be our little secret because he looks like burnt chicken to me....her face got all serious and she got quiet. I turned around and it was like I spoke of the devil because there he was right behind me. I mean we have celebrities in and out of the club but I didn't expect that to ever happen. I mean seriously want are the chances like two hundred million to one? It was not as bad as it could have turned out, he just smiled and had me give him a stage dance then a forty-five-minute lap dance followed by two peep shows. He got himself off while looking at me, tipped me five thousand dollars, told me I inspired him and left happy. So, although I was busted poking fun at him, he didn't care and remained kind and humble. I should say he inspired me, even if I was just joking and teasing Persway to make her laugh, it wasn't very kind of me.

Sometimes I really wonder what or who I am becoming; slowly dancing is chewing away at what tattered fabric I have left of myself, trying to swallow my soul. I am just becoming a super bitch because to make better money at work I have to be a bitch. I even sometimes feel like I should bring my cauldron to properly perform my bitchcraft, it seems like it would be the perfect place to stash my nightly earnings. I don't know what is wrong with people, whatever happen to wanting to be treated with kindness and respect?

I hope that soon I will have enough money saved to just move out and still have enough to give me a good year cushion to find a job. I would also like and get back to school. The online classes are easier, but I have to cram my weekly classes into the day or two I take off every week and I am getting burnt out. I could probably cut my hours to working single shifts now though, I have a steady flow of regulars and I making plenty of money off of them. I don't know why God doesn't just show me the way out of this life path and open a new door for me. Of course, God has really been drifting and floating farther from me these days. I can't let go of the anger and hurt at the fact that he continues to allow all these and things to keep happening in my life. I am hopeful that I will be able to find my way back to God soon and life will get better. I know it will if God can only forgive me enough to hear my prayers.

Well I had better get back to sleep after putting some work in on classes I am beat. I will have a full three hours of sleep before I have to get up and get ready for work, and I have to repeat it all until the end of forever.

CHAPTER 37

HUSTLING HARD

As the days passed over the past week, the customers just seemed to get stranger and stranger. This really sexy man dressed in a business suit walked in around three in the afternoon, and he went to the front and paid for an hour lap dance. When I took him back to a private lap dance booth he was very softly spoken and just wanted me to talk to him with my top off. He complained about work in the film industry and his wife and kids and I listened. Then when his hour of talking was up he tipped me and requested a peep show. "Ok so far so good!" That was until he took a flash light out of his pocket to hold in his mouth so I could see him jerking off. I lied and told him the flash light wasn't helping to see anything, that because my piece of glass was the one tinted it wasn't working. I acted really disappointed and played it up to make him excited. So, he ended up buying two peep shows to get himself off and just wanted me to lay my back against the mirror behind me; with my legs open, no panties on but everything else still on. He was so proud of the massive load he left on my glass and he wanted to know if I was impressed too. After I came out of my booth the bouncer held the door open on the customer's side and stood between us so I was safe while I inspected it, I lied and said it was so hot and so sexy that he left me such a huge load, he gave me a bigger tip. Then he asked me if I wanted to choke him with my leg. That is around the time he got bounced out of the club.

After that last customer I have had enough. I was ready for a day off. But then this guy comes in right after him, thinking that giving me a dollar every time I walk by will get me to sit and talk to him. He said, "Hey honey, I have been giving you money all night why won't you come talk to me?" I laughed a little and responded, "First of all don't call me honey and second of all if you want to talk to me buy a dance." Then I turned to walk my next customer to his lap dance booth. The customer I was currently with was a regular and a coke head. He does line after line the entire time he is with you and buys hour after hour of lap dances. He worked the dancers hard to keep him entertained but he tipped extremely well. So, after five long hours of lap dancing on this guy I came out to see the other man still hasn't left. He waited five hours to buy a lap dance with me. Then he just wanted to rub my feet while he talked and then he tipped me. It was so strange at first but then he started talking about his dead wife and how lonely he was. It was sad really and I felt bad I had to hustle him so hard but I was working and I couldn't just talk to him and lose out on money. So, while I put my shoes back on, I talked him into another lap dance after he tipped me fifty for the first one. I told him to get a fifteen minute instead of a thirty (because that was all I needed to get him to buy some peep shows.) Then I had to explain to him that the lap dances at the club were sold in fifteen-minute increments and he went off and came back with his lap dance ticket. The bouncer just smiled and winked at me because he loved watching me hustle, he said I made it look easy. Once back in the lap dance booth, I took my strappy stripper dress down and left it around my waist and hips, exposing the naked flesh of my breasts and dancing seductively in his lap. Using my leg against his I am able to create and illusionary sensation of desire. Without ever touching or grinding directly on his crotch I could see the power of my lure started seductively asking him if he wanted a peep show. At first, he told me no, but then he looked down at his pants and his boner that was constricted with in and then he looked back at me, and I asked "Don't you want to see all of me? Don't you want to see my tight pussy?" As soon as I saw his jaw drop and his eyes widen, I knew I hooked him. After the lap dance, he followed me back to the peep show booth, I explained how it worked and then I went in and locked my door and held my key to the reader. When the curtain went up, he looked really nervous, but as my breasts were exposed, he got more relaxed and melted into the chair. The entire time my mind was telling me how wrong it was for me to take advantage of a man who just told me he lost his wife two years ago, and who hasn't seen a naked woman since. But I just kept pushing though. When I took my dress all the way down and I was just in a G-string he pulled his penis from his pants. Then I took the panties off too and sat with my back arched half way off the platform in my booth with my hips tucked up and spread my legs. I use my hands to cup my flesh around my nipples and slapped myself right above my vagina giving the illusion that I was teasing and touching my naughty bits. After all, that is what strippers become good at, illusions and hypnosis. Then the curtain dropped and he put more money in the machine. When the curtain when back up I felt guilty for hustling this guy. When I looked down and saw all the tip money on the floor in my booth under the tip slot I had to do something to feel less guilty. So, although I normal charge the men to speak to them on the phone while they look at me, I picked up the phone and started talking all the dirty talk he wanted to hear. When he was able to climax, I felt a little less guilty about the last tip that fell through the slot. I don't know what is going on with me but I really need to get out of my own head, hustling these guys is how I survive, how I pay my bills, how I will get away from Corey.

The last day I put myself on to work for this week seemed like it would never end. A new girl started and Persway and I are the only two girls being nice to her. Alice is not super pretty and she seems a bit shy. She is literally one of those comic book nerds, all she has been talking about is Comic con and Star Wars, and I seriously don't know what she is talking about. She signed herself on to be paid by the hour as an employee of the club instead of an independent contractor like she should have. "And here I thought that nerds were smart." Persway and I are really concerned that she won't make it. So, we try to give her some tips and tell her to ditch the pumps and get dancing stilettos because they make your legs and ass look better and they grip the slick tile we walk and dance on.

She is too shy for that though. So, she sits and watches us take turns dancing on the stage and taking customers back for lap dances and peep shows. Finally, a regular sees the new fresh meat and asks Alice for a peep show. When Alice comes back out to the floor, she is Casper white and looks like she might cry. So, we ask her what happened and why she seems so shaken, then she tells us that when she took her clothes off so did the customer and he had jacked off while looking at her naked. We didn't say anything right away just looked at her stunned by her reaction, and then we asked her what she thought was going to happen. She broken down because she said all the signs on the guys side and on the doors to the video booths all said that it wasn't allowed. We kind of laughed and told her they all do it and they tip better. Besides, why do you think we all have tip the janitor every night? She was overly shy and such a prude, I asked her why she wanted a job here and the poor thing said she was trying to impress her boyfriend. I knew in my gut she wasn't cut out for this work, so I helped her pack her things and saw her out. I told her that if her boyfriend couldn't love her for who she is inside then he didn't deserve her. What I really wanted to say was, don't let your nerdy boyfriend push you to do things you are uncomfortable with, because no matter what you do that won't make his dick any bigger. But I knew that was just the bitch inside of me that wanted to say that, but she reminded me of who I really use to be. Helping save her from being broken, jaded and callused by men helped me realize that somewhere under all this bullshit and ugly the happy girl in me, is trapped waiting to be freed. I just couldn't watch other girls who are still happy and innocent (as they should be) get crushed until their hearts turned cold and as black as mine.

CHAPTER 38

ROBBING THE BANK OF GWEN

The past month has been nothing short of a struggle to get through. I have to keep pushing myself to go to work in that toxic place.

When I got back to my apartment after work at one am, I walked into to a scene that made me panic. Everything was ransacked and gone through, my books and movies were all over the floor, couch cushions removed, my clothes scattered from my dresser, and closet in complete disarray. Who would have done this…? the apartments are gated.

I needed to find my cats first and then maybe I would call the police. As I was looking for my beloved fur babies, I noticed the loose board on the book shelves was ajar. My heart sank into the pit of my stomach and I started to cry. Then it hit me, where is Corey? I know this had to be him there was no way any robber would have only taken money or even thought to look for a money stash. Plus, what robber shuts and locks your door after they rob you. That is literally like saying, "oh hey sorry I had to rob you but let me keep what is left safe and lock up for you!" As that thought flew through my mind I was able to calm down a little knowing that some stranger wasn't in my apartment was a small comfort. I was still really pissed that Corey took my money and why was even looking for it in the first place?

After finding my cats locked in the drawers of my dresser, I felt a surge of extreme anger take over. I grabbed my keys and headed to the only place I knew that creep would be, the bar on the Sunset strip. Sure, enough when I got there, he was buying rounds for all his friends on the patio bar with my money! I couldn't take this or allow myself to be ok with the scene that I was witnessing unfold before my eyes. He has poor dumb groupies hanging on his arms and smiling like he is something important, I wish they would just take him. I wouldn't be that lucky, that would require him to get the hell out of my life and he seems dead set on destroying it.

With all the courage I could muster I walked right up to Corey and confront him face to face. I demanded to know why he would steal from me but all he has to say to me about it is, "Bitch you were stealing from me, you know better. What made you think you could hide money from me?" I couldn't believe what he was saying, did he really think it was his money? So, with everyone now watching us I calmly tell him I worked for that money and that if he wanted money, he would have to get a job and work for it. With that he laughed and grabbed the girl on his right arm and told me he was going to Vegas to have a good time. He yelled at me to get out of his face and stop nagging. Then he turned and walked out of the bar with the woman he grabbed, got into her car and left. I was angry he was taking my money but I couldn't careless that he was going to Vegas, any time away from him is welcomed. Since it was close to last call, I went home to get some sleep to be ready for work the following day.

CHAPTER 39

CATCHING A RAPIST

When I got to work, I was not rested or prepared enough for the day or week for that matter ahead of me. It started out pretty normal, stage dancing, lap dances, peep shows and happy customers. Then Emily came in and told Persway and I about some serial rapists that has been targeting strippers in our area. So, we were on high alert always looking to see if any of the men fit the description; suddenly work was more stressful than ever.

Just as I was settling into a nice flow of working and passing the hours, a new face pops into the club. He looks really paranoid and keeps fidgeting around. When I approach him, he says he wants a peep show, so I am more than willing, thinking maybe he is just nervous. Then he explains he will wait for a few other men to have peep shows first, I don't know what his deal is but I have customers waiting for my time. After a few peep shows I start to wonder what he is waiting for, and why he keeps checking the booth when the men walk out. I just brush the thought away because I have a regular who loves to have me sit topless with my dress around my waist no panties and my high heeled feet spread open and resting on my booth platform. I am just thankful to have a regular that was a creature of habit come in, it makes my job easier and I don't have to hustle as hard because he knows the drill. He usually takes about four peep shows and always cums all over my glass. It is pretty gross but I am just thankful I am not the one who has to clean the booths after every customer. As I walk out to gather the next customer the new guy stops the janitor from cleaning the room and tells me he is ready. I am a bit confused but agree to the peep show. As soon as the curtain goes up this guy starts jerking himself off which is pretty standard, but once he comes on the load of cum left by my last customer, he bends down and licks every drop of it up. I really thought I was going to blow chunks, but I had to keep cool because they can't know we can see them. I mean come on if you are into licking another mans' cum up, why are you watching a woman dance and pleasuring yourself to her image? It really made me sick. When the janitor came to clean the glass before my next customer, he apologized for not being able to tell me that guy was a cum licker. He told me he hadn't seen him in the club for two years but warned me we would see more of him for telling me, but I was now was wrestling with the idea of that man becoming one of my regulars.

As if the week couldn't get any crazier, one of my regulars came in while I was entertaining a peep show and started going insane. He was pounding on the booth doors and shouting about how I was his and that he would kill the guy looking at me. I had to apologize to the poor guy and then I had to calm my regular down while walking over to security. I felt bad but this was no way to act and I wasn't his or anyone's for that matter. I was an exotic dancer in a club. These guys really can scare me sometimes, they really buy into the fantasy they want created. Clearly that is not normal and not all guys go postal like this or become obsessed, but a good number of them do. Once the customer was asked to leave and then escorted out, I had to get the club to comp my peep show customer a peep show which did not make me happy. It meant that I was basically giving him the second show for free. I was really upset about it until he tipped me three hundred dollars for fighting the club to comp him the second show. They didn't want to because he only had two minutes left out of the seven, but I wasn't ok with that. The fact that because security wasn't fast enough to defuse the situation and it killed his experience was unacceptable. That would look bad on me and I am counting on making as many regulars as I can for constant income flow and increases. Things were slowly starting to get more and more crazy and I was just trying to hang in there.

Two weeks into the month and all the dancers are on high alert; the rapist they have been looking for is defiantly in our club. He is so strange and we are trying to keep him happy and watch each other while we wait for the police to get here; damn Hollywood traffic. This guy is really pawing the dancers and offering us money to go home with him, I can't believe that security hasn't kicked him out. Then Persway comes over and tells me they called the police but we have to keep him busy, nobody goes outside and lap dances happen with curtain open.

The man all the girls are sure is the rapist, asks me for a peep show so I accept his request. I am a bit scared and also thankful to be behind a locked door but I can't help the sick feeling curling in my stomach, the fear and my adrenaline are getting the best of me. His eyes are cold and filled with some kind of wicked desire, he keeps licking his lips and thrusting into the glass. What seems like an eternity later the cops open his side of the peep show booth and arrest him? I am so glad for that and a relief washes over me.

A few uneventful days pass and the girls and I are praying for the club to pick up. It is hard to pass the time on a double shift with a scatter of customers. I just try to remind myself that it is close to the Thanksgiving holiday and people are just probably with their families.

CHAPTER 40

JOURNAL ENTRY

I know it has been awhile since I last made an entry, but that is because I have been trying to forget the holiday season. First Thanksgiving was a complete and utter disaster. I picked up the ham to bring to my parent's house but Corey made us so late it wasn't fully heated on time. Then Corey kept trying to keep me from talking to any of my family alone, he was always standing there like I might say something. At the end of dinner, he was in such a rush to get out of my parents' house and back to the apartment I almost didn't have time to say goodbye to my mom. He really made quite the scene.

After Thanksgiving I thought Christmas Eve would have gone a little better at my parents' house. I could not have been more wrong! Corey was coked out of his mind most of the holiday season and he was acting like a complete jackass. After Christmas Eve dinner was eaten, he was in such a rush to leave he started yanking me by the arm to the door. I mean he wasn't even letting me get my coat and purse and went as far as to pull me away from talking to my uncle. My dad kind of got in his face about it and asked him what his problem was. After that he backed off a bit, but I could see the rage in his eyes. The coke was really escalating his anger more than usual.

Christmas was not much better, my parents got me a really thoughtful gift box of new makeup items and skin care. I was so happy; they even got Corey some gifts. He was just completely rude and embarrassing as usual. When he decided it was time to leave before Christmas dinner my mom started crying asking my dad to do something. So, my dad stepped in and said that he would bring me home later. I told my dad it was fine that I didn't want him to drive up and back all that way in holiday traffic, it would take him hours. The most painful thing for me was seeing the light of discovery on the faces of my family and the tears streaming down my mother's face. The cat is out of the bag, now my entire family knows about my abusive "boyfriend" they may not know all the details, but they saw enough to know there is abuse going on.

I think after all of this writing and going back through it the one consistent thing I see is negativity. Negative, in what happens in my life being more impactful in my life than the positive, negative in the way I keep blaming God. I just need to figure out how to get positivity in my life. Again, something is shifting in me and I am just praying that is it a good thing this time. I don't think I can handle much more of the ugliness surrounding me in life. With all that being said I am so thankful to Tammy for gifting me the journals I write in every day. The writing has ended up being more therapeutic and problem solving than I ever thought it would be, it lets me get everything out and reflect at the same time. It is really funny how sometimes your friends just know what is good for you and what you need, even when you don't see it.

I know I have only been working at the strip club for about six months but I need out of it. I think I am pretty close to having enough money saved to move out away from Corey. Or maybe I am just becoming brave enough to jump ship and push through no matter what. Only the Lord knows what the future holds.

CHAPTER 41

GOOD SENSE OF HUMOR

After the holidays had passed, the club picked up again, and things were going good. With customers flowing back into the club, so was the money; and I couldn't wait to get the nest egg to the goal amount that felt most comfortable to me. I had begun counting the time I had left trapped with Corey, by the days no longer weeks. The men in the club were cheering and throwing money at me while I was dancing on stage to entertain the crowd. I was waiting my turn to get back on the floor to lap dances and peep shows, and then it happened....when I flipped on the pole my stiletto flew off and hit a customer in the face. I have never been more embarrassed, how could that have even happened? I am glad the customer had a good sense of humor and laughed it off, and then he even tipped me for breaking his nose. I really felt awful, but all the girls thought it was the funniest thing ever.

When all the laughing died down, we had a group of young eighteen-year-old guys come in. They were so nervous and didn't know what to expect, so I took them one at a time for a lap dance and then a peep show. A few of them decided that the fifteen-minute lap dance was not long enough and got a thirty-minute to follow. I didn't expect that they would cum in their pants, it was funny and somewhat cute considering there is no direct crotch grinding. The others didn't last but seconds in the peep show booth, and it was refreshing to see guys that weren't completely ruined by their perversions in the club for a change.

I am glad that even though the customer flow has picked back up, that I was able to catch a break on gaining any new strange or uncomfortable new customers. All of the new and old perversions are really getting to me and wearing me down mentally and visually. Some days I even catch myself feeling envy for the deaf and mute, which I should be feeling quite the opposite. All the strange guys do the nasty stuff you wish you could unsee. All of the uncomfortable guys try to talk to you as if you are on a date because they don't do well with women. So the average man, who is still a pig, is better than the other two customer types.

CHAPTER 42

FIGHTING BACK

This life is really wearing on me. Corey is deeper into drugs and drinking than ever. He completely freaked out because his friend Jason came to my twenty-fourth birthday party at the bar. Jason was like all the other guests celebrating with me, he wished me happy birthday, gave me a hug, bought me a drink and shared some laughs. So naturally, I took a pretty good beating for it. Only this time I was able to use the freezer door and then a frying pan to hit him in self-defense. I was at first surprised when he started in on me while I was getting some water, but then I was thankful to be in the kitchen with tools to help defend myself.

Corey was in shock when I swung open the freezer door and it hit him in the face; I actually think the initial shock was felt more by me considering I was just trying to put something in between us. It was really on for me after that, I felt a surge of courage and fight I was not accustomed to: I followed the hit with the freezer door with a swing of the frying pan from the dish strainer. I hit him over the head with it and knocked him out. I didn't know why I was so calm about it when I stepped over him with my water to go to the shower and get ready for bed, but it just felt freeing. There was no doubt that I was becoming stronger and I was changing for the better, I could feel it all through my body. I just had better things to worry about, than about my abuser knocked out on the kitchen floor. I needed to worry about making my life happy and myself happy for a change.

Work has been really wearing me out. Emotionally and mentally I feel so drained. I had a regular customer come in and during his third lap dance he tried to pull me down onto him. I shouted at him to stop but he wouldn't let go of me. The bouncer was not coming, I didn't know where he went: All I did know was that I was topless and alone with a man that was trying to overpower me, to do God knows what. I was trying to pry away from him, but being topless left me feeling really vulnerable and afraid. I quickly learn just how warranted my fear was when I asked him to let me go. He lunged forward taking my nipple into his mouth and sucking on it before biting down so hard he drew blood. I reached down for the shoe on my foot and yelled at him to smile and wave at the cameras, before hitting him as hard as I could in the head. He let me out of his grip and held his hand to his bleeding head as I ran out of the booth. It all happen in what seemed like lightning fast speed, and I was really shaken by it. I was extremely upset that the bouncer walked away while I was doing a lap dance. He knew that he was supposed to stay in the lap dance booth area while girls were doing lapdances. The security walked the rest of the club and we didn't have a door bouncer because there was no bar. When the cops got to the club the customer was being held in the managers' office. The cops reviewed the tapes, took a police report and arrested him, but it didn't make me feel any better. This job was just not safe and I needed out.

A week later all the girls were talking. The regular pimp showed up a few days ago; I learned from the whispers and talk buzzing around the club, he recruited Lilly. I was so sad for her because I really thought she would finish school and make it. I was here today when she got caught having sex with customers in their cars. She was giving them lap dances and peep shows to help sell herself. They fired her while she was being escorted out in handcuffs after they called the police to arrest her. I wonder what is going to happen to her son now that she is going to have to register as a sex offender, and I wonder if her husband knew what was going on. I think one of the coke dealers that comes through got her hooked on that too. I told her drugs are not acceptable forms of payment and to always get *cash* tips. She was just so sure that she could sell them and make more money than getting a straight cash tip. I am sure she was using because I don't think she would have ever put such shame on herself by having to be added to the sex offender registry list. She always seemed so much more concerned with keeping her work a secret and private, all so her son would never find out and never be ashamed or embarrassed of her.

It has been wet from the rains this season and the customers can't seem to dry their shoes, on the rug provided properly before walking through the entrance to the club. So of course, in a rush to get back to working, I slip on the wet tile walkway leading from the store to the club and sprang my ankle and break my foot. Just my luck! I have to leave my shift early not to return for the night, I have to stay off my foot for the rest of the night and lose money. I am just glad that I was able to get the doctor to agree to give me a doctor's note to return to work with guide lines.

After making sure I have my doctor's note is in my bag, I return to work the next day with Advil, an ace bandage and some cute fuzzy socks. I pair my socks with boy shorts over my G-string and a white a- shirt aka wifebeater over my bra and braid my hair into pigtails. I am worried about not being as appealing to the customers, but I find they love it. The customers tell me they like the innocent little girl look I have taken on and it even makes some of my co-workers mad because their regulars are getting dances and shows with me. I only feel mildly bad because I can't force the customers to go with the other girls or turn down shows and dances, plus I am making so much money. Even if Corey is taking almost all of it this gives me a new opportunity to save.

The customers are getting more and more needy and interesting. I had a few couples come in over the past few weeks. At first, I didn't know what to expect, couples would come in here and there but it always kept me on my toes. When a couple comes into the club you never know which way things are going to go, sometimes the one partner would be really hyped up and the other would ride that wave. Other times you would get the couples that started fighting over jealousy. Then you had the couples looking to build sexual appetite. They would always keep me busy doing lap dances, until the husband or boyfriend was ready to move over to the peep show booths. They would both strip down and fuck each other while the husband or boyfriend was talking to me on the phone set, and staring at me nude on the other side of the glass the entire time. Asking me if I loved his cock and how he was fucking me, when in reality he wasn't. It was a strange way to fulfill a fantasy and really hard to act like I was blind to what they were doing. Not that I couldn't tell anyway by the heavy panting, but they tipped extremely well so I didn't complain. Then I wondered if any of these people noticed all the cameras, there were no blind spots in the club, not even in the bathrooms, it was for our safety. I guess as a dancer I just figured it had to be general knowledge that when you walk into a strip club you are agreeing to being filmed even in the privacy of the bathrooms. Now when I say the bathrooms, I mean there were cameras facing the door and sinks, the actual toilets or urinals were not filmed. The idea was to always be able to see who was going in and out to ensure the girls weren't being dragged or followed in by the customers.

CHAPTER 43

JOURNAL ENTRY

I am starting to worry about Persway, she missed two shifts at the club and she isn't answering her phone or responding to text messages. I know that her boyfriend is abusive and controlling like Corey is to me, so maybe she is just laying low after a fight between them. I just have this really bad gut feeling that something is very wrong because she isn't even reachable by phone, she always at least calls me back. I will say a little prayer for her and if she misses another shift, I will call the club owner David and ask him to come in and make a call to the police. I know when girls just decide to quit, some of them just stop showing up for their week's shifts, but she would have told me if that was the case. We became pretty close and put ourselves on the schedule for the same dates and shifts to work together.

Speaking of being worried about people I am really concerned about the spiral Lilly is on. I heard that CPS took her son and placed him with her sister. I guess the pain of losing her son because she is now a registered sex offender and had to take parenting classes and drug counseling, she just lost it. She has been picked up twice in the past few weeks for prostitution, and the week before that was bailed out on charges of theft and drug possession. I was really hoping and praying she would get it together, she had a chance of getting her son back because she wasn't charged with any sex crimes involving a minor. There were also no findings of abuse, neglect or endangerment toward her son. It is all just so heart wrenching. I suppose that the light in all of it, is that her son is with family even given the circumstances.

Everything that has been going on around me and in my life has made me feel like I need to pull back on the reigns a bit. I don't want to spiral so far down that I can't dig myself back out. I have been talking to Andy again and we have really just clicked right back in sync and we have a beautiful comfortable friendship. He makes me laugh and I am smiling again and it feels good. I am glad that this time there is no romantic pressure and things are just easy going. I love my girls and we have so much fun going out and laughing together and doing what girls do, but there is just something that is so much easier flowing in a friendship with the opposite sex. Or maybe it is just my imagination and the only difference is my preference in eye candy, and I say preference because my friends are really beautiful.

Anyway, I am going to quit the club at the end of

the month. I have to get away from the cliental. Working there has real warped my perception of men. I find I have had sexual aversions in talking with my girlfriends about men and who they are finding attractive. Even the most gorgeous of men don't do anything for my libido. At first, I just thought it was because I had no intentions of having sex with anyone until I get away from Corey and find "the one." That is not the issue though. Every time I see a man all I do is ponder about what kind of sick sexual desires he has. Does he like to sit on giant dildos, does he drink his own semen, does he like to have a woman act like a girl under 15 and call him daddy? If it isn't that, when men come over to talk to me when I am out with the girls, I feel like a prey animal being hunted by a hungry wolf, sneaky and sly just trying to feed the hunger of the moment. Then when I am back at work, I imagine myself and my co-workers as innocent sheep trying to run and dodge the paws and gnashing teeth of the wolves that are trying to pounce on us. I always feel like I am only one foot away from being slaughter by the pack.

So yeah, I am pretty sure it is time to just quit!

CHAPTER 44

THE DARK, JUST GOT DARKER

After just about every single peep show these men want to shake the hands of the dancers, they must still have a lack of blood to the brain, considering they just jerked off while looking at us. It is the most disgusting thing to have them expect us to shake their dirty hands after that. We of course just wave and say thank you or pretend to cough in our hand to avoid the handshake. There were of course a few times a dancer would slip up and in a moment of absent mindedness would shake hands; and then after the customer walked away, they ran to the bathroom screaming to scrub their hands. I hated how these men just didn't seem to mind trying to shake our hands. Just because they wiped "clean" with a tissue didn't make it any less revolting. Did they not consider that a dry tissue did not have the same germ and residue removing impact as a good old fashion hand washing, there was just no substitute for soap and water. So, I brought a pair of kitchen gloves to work because I fancied myself funny. After every peep show when the customer wanted a hand shake, I would put one on and offer to shake their hand. They always got a puzzled look on their faces and asked what I was doing, I simply said, "weren't you just beating your meat in there? I don't want to have your dick all over my hands." I think it was safe to say that I was fed up. It was easier to tell how done I was with the sheer stupidity of men that lost all blood flow in their brains because it was flowing to their other head, because when they would all ask if I could see them, I rolled my eyes and ignored the question. Instead of playing coy I finally got so sick of it that I told one guy, "Look, can you see yourself in the mirror behind me?" When he said yeah, I told him, "think about that!" At least I got a good laugh about the puzzled thought that washed over his face. He ended up having to buy extra peep shows because he was working so hard to figure out what I had just said to him. This poor fool, the blood flow was fighting between his two heads.

The day I knew I needed to quit was when I came in for the morning shift with Emily and there was this God-awful smell outside. We always parked our cars out back behind the club to enter through the club's direct entrance, the two club parking lots were separated by an alley way and at the back of the second lot was the club and store dumpsters. Normally a slight sour smell in the air on a warm day would have been normal considering; but we rarely had food waste that was even tossed out, and this was not the smell of rotting trash. This smelled more like a decomposing animal, but stronger and more pungent than I have ever smelled. We couldn't help but look around for it. As we were getting closer and closer to the dumpster in the back of the lot, the smell was growing stronger the closer we got. Emily stopped dead in her tracks in front of me and let out this blood curdling scream. As she doubled over to vomit, I saw Persway behind the dumpster covered in flies. Her body looked like it was cut open from her vagina to her sternum and the ring finger on her left hand was gone.

My head was awash in a sea of rushing thoughts a mixture of memories and questions. My heart was racing and my breathing was erratic, I went it to a hyperventilation attack that made me feel dizzy and I dropped to my knees to avoid falling. It was only when I was able to focus my breathing and calm down that I heard the officer talking to me, "miss, can you walk? I need you to come with me, I have a few questions." I just nodded in response to the officer and stood up and followed her to the other side of the alley parking lot. The officer asked me to sit on the bench next to Emily and told me she would be right back. When she walked away, I wondered how long ago they got here and why I didn't hear them pull up or even notice.

When the officer finished talking to her partner she comes back over to Emily and I and starts, her standard line of questioning. "How long have you worked here, did you know the victim well, did any one seem to have an issue with her at the club, did you see anything unusual, when did you last speak to the victim." All the questions that came from the officer's mouth were answered with NOs, until she asked, if either one of use recognized the murder weapon and she held up a bag with a bloody knife in it. I froze with fear because I did recognize it. I said, "that is the knife I bought her for her birthday two weeks ago, it was the one she said she wanted to carry in her bag for protection." The fear that this was somehow my fault was filling my mind, because maybe if I didn't get her that knife, she would not have had a weapon on her for some creep to use to hurt her and kill her. The walls I had around my heart crumpled as my heart exploded from the pain of that realization. The officer asked us if we knew about her personal life outside of the club and if there was anyone, we felt she had problems with, so I filled the officer in on what I knew about her relationship with her boyfriend. Then before the officer let us go, she said "one last question. Have either of you seen or heard from the bouncer Fabian? It seems that he has not shown up to work this morning and nobody can seem to get in touch with him." Of course, we both said, "no" we didn't mingle with the bouncers or security guards outside of the club so we had no clue where he was or how to find him. "Go ask the janitor", I said. The officer just smiled and said, "We are asking everyone."

CHAPTER 45

JOURNAL ENTRY

My eyes are red and swollen from crying, I have been crying all morning and most of the afternoon. I still can't believe that Persway is gone, I don't think I will ever get the sight of her dead bloody body out of my mind. I took a shower when I got back to the apartment but I still can smell the sent of death and decomposing flesh all around me. I think it is just my imagination though because I can't stop thinking about her. I really wish I didn't buy her that knife, it was such a bad idea. I wonder if the police have spoken to her boyfriend yet or if they have found Fabian. I wish I could find out anything but they will only release information to immediate family. I am sick of losing people and this just isn't fair to Persway or anyone around her. She was so beautiful from the inside out, God I wish I didn't just write that, I made myself sound like I am not being sincere but I am. Emily called me just a little while ago and told me she heard that they are looking into all possibilities, including the possibility of her murder being a hate crime. The words "hate crime" made me hang my head with sorrow. At least if it was a crime of passion, she was not being murder because someone was raging a war against a singular group of people for the pigment in their skin. She was kind and beautiful she had a loving generous heart and she deserved to be loved. What am I saying I did and do love her.

I told David the club owner, that I was finished and would not be working at the club any longer, he told me I had better finish out my work hours because I was on the schedule. He told me in a callus manner, that with Persway not coming in for the same shifts he wasn't willing to risk losing the money. Can you believe the nerve of that prick? I am mourning the loss of my friend and co-worker whose death was most likely directly caused by one of the creeps that frequent the club, and he is basically demanding I work anyway. I guess I can see it a little from his stand point he owns a business and let's face it businesses are in the business or making money.

So, I am at least on notice with the club, now all I have to do is find a place of my own so I can get away from Corey. It is time to start fresh and praise the Lord for everyday that I wake up alive and well. I have to find a better way, I can't keep wading through the negativity I am surrounded in. If I keep putting this off or don't get out of it now soon, I will be drowning in it.

I hate to write and run, but Tammy is here. She came by to talk while we bake and drink wine. While I try to keep my mind off of all this horrible pain and loss.

CHAPTER 46

DESPERATE TO LEAVE

I hate that I have to finish out my week here at the club. When I got to work today and parked in the parking lot I couldn't get out of the car, I was just too traumatized and upset. I sat in my car with my eyes closed trying to talk myself into getting out of the car and walking into the club, but I just didn't have it in me. It was not until the security guard Evan came and knocked on my window, that I felt ok to get out of the car. I am just finished with all the drama and evil this place seems to spawn. The money isn't worth it. At least David and Miguel have started enforcing the rules about the bouncers and guards walking the girls to and from their cars. I am happy that the other girls will remain safe for it, but I am pissed the rule wasn't enforced with such an iron fist before Persway was murdered.

As the week wears on, I just settle into the normal routine of hustling and try to push everything else from my mind. As I am doing a peep show, I see something in this customer's hand but I need a better look, it looks wrapped in tape. Then it hits me, "Oh my God he has a camera, are you fucking kidding me? He has been here for hours getting peep shows, I can't believe the other girls didn't catch this." I yank my door open and holler for the club owner David (thank God he is here today.) I am pounding on the door as David comes rushing in to find out what is going on. I can't believe he is playing dumb. He can see and hear every inch of this club including inside both the dancer and customer sides of the peep show booths, from his office; which is why he heard me and came running. I bet he was too busy perving on all us girls to see that this jackass has a camera. Once David unlocks the customer's door with his master keys, security wrestles him to the ground taking the camera. He had photos of all the girls and a list about how much he thought he could sell us for. It was so scary and I was glad this was my last night. David didn't care about the dancers, all he cared about was his profits and getting his cut of our lap dances and peep shows.

Once I gathered myself, I changed and collected my peep show and lap dance money from the front. Then I said my goodbyes to all the girls and had security walk me to my car, and I didn't look back, I was so done.

CHAPTER 47

THE LAST STRAW

When I got back to the apartment and put the key in the door, I got the feeling someone was watching me. I stopped and turned around leaving my keys hang from the doorknob, as I slowly took in the scene around me, I didn't see any one. Now that I was officially creeped out, I spun back around and unlocked the doorknob lock quickly followed by the dead bolt; as I pushed the door open, I could see that the apartment was in shambles again. "Fucking Corey man!" As I walked in, I stepped over the mess and checked my money stash, it was untouched. I found it strange that Corey would trash the place but then leave the money. "What was he after?" As I mauled over the mystery in my head, I located my cats and then began to clean up the mess. It was not until I had finished cleaning and then sat down to write in my journal like I did everyday that I noticed my journal was missing. I looked through the apartment just to be sure that I had not miss placed it while I was cleaning the aftermath of Corey's apartment search. It was not in the apartment.

As I sat crying on the couch Corey came in. He asked me what was going on and asked me why I was crying. I looked up at him in disbelief and said, "are you kidding me? You took my journal, you just stole all of my inner most private thoughts. Where is it you jerk?"

"I didn't take your journal Gwen"

"Then where is it?"

"I don't know, I would not take it. I know how much it means to you and I just would not take it."

"You expect me to believe that, you will take my money but not my journal? You hit me and force sex on me, but taking my journal is out of the question for you? What kind of fool do you take me for?"

"Man fuck this, I will be back tomorrow. I said I didn't touch your stupid journal and that is exactly what I mean."

After Corey stormed out, slamming the door behind him I called my parents and asked them to come get me in the morning. I had no choice I needed help to get out as soon as possible, taking my personal thoughts was the last straw. I used my writing to reflect on myself and my life, to see my mistakes and look for the patterns to break. He didn't just take my journal he stole the hope of me learning where I am fumbling in life. This really is the straw that broke the camel's back because I hate him through and through. As I pack my things to be ready to move in the morning, I tell myself out loud what I need to do to have a clean break from Corey. I don't care how many messages he leaves apologizing, I am not going to take his calls or respond his texts. All the words that come out of his mouth are lies and his tears are that of a crocodile, he is a snake in the grass.

First thing this morning I called mom on her cell to find out if they were on their way. I tried to stay calm on the phone but the tears came faster than I could choke them back. When I hung up the phone, I started double checking that I had packed all my belongings because mom and dad were on their way to get me. Again, I was leaving without saying a word to Corey, or at least that was the plan. Corey came back to the apartment and caught me in the middle of packing, and started yelling and crying. I wasn't falling for his pseudo tears and just simply told him I was moving back home to get back on my feet. I was glad he started packing too and was able to purchase a plane ticket back to his home town in New Orleans. Maybe he could be happy being a washed-up musician there. He called Jason and asked him to drive the car down to New Orleans next week since he planned on driving a rental down anyway on a road trip with some of the guys. It was all settled and I felt freedom at my fingertips.

When mom and dad got me all packed into the car and we were on our way, I was so thankful. The fur babies even seemed to be excited to get away from the dark cloud we were living in. I didn't look back once while we drove away and arriving home was almost magical, I felt like the princess that had to be saved from the fire breathing dragon. As I unpacked, I let the thought of me in a dark tower wearing a beautiful renaissance style gown, with a giant, beautiful but ferocious dragon guarding the perimeter. Sweep over me, and it brought me to a giggling fit. I didn't take too much of my stuff when I moved back with Corey so unpacking was not such a big deal and I was done fairly quickly. By the time I finished putting everything in its place and showering off, my cats were settled in my bed fast asleep. It was clear by the sight of them so soundly asleep they were just as happy to be home as I was. They didn't even stir when I came into the room from the shower.

Once I was settled in back at home, I felt safe and happy and I thanked God. I was happy to see Will again too. He had just finished college and was excited to have a new job lined up. I only had a few months left before I was done with my college courses as well. I told him what a struggle it was to take classes slower or online so I could do classes in between work and he totally understood the stress. But then he asked me if that was all that was going on. I couldn't tell him about all the abuse, I knew he would hunt Corey down and do something stupid. I really missed my family and maybe they were what I needed to heal.

Within weeks I was hanging out with my friends again and I sincerely felt really happy. I even got to see Andy when he was home for a visit. I was super excited to see him face to face and be hugged like I mattered. It had been a little over a year that I spent with Corey being isolated, but it felt like I was living in a time warp where time moved slower. I went out and just let loose and had some drinks, went dancing, I talked to men and other human beings without the fear of punishment or embarrassment. I went to the movies for the first time in a year and I got to pick the movie without being yelled at. I bought popcorn lots of popcorn and drinks. I went to the beach and rode the waves and soaked up the freedom and the happiness I felt. It is funny how being kept from simple things, even for just a year can really make you love them with a new-found intensity.

The waves of tension back home at my parents' house, was a bit stressful with all the fighting between my parents. All the fighting and yelling just caused fights to spread. It made no sense because most of the fighting started from all the chronic complaining. It was like being caught in town with constant bad weather. So, I spent a lot of time listening and observing. I got a new journal and started keeping my notes, thoughts and reflections pouring out onto paper. Writing it all down and then reading it out loud and hearing it were really helping me see from a new perspective. Maybe the problem has been right in front of me the entire time and this process will help me pinpoint it.

CHAPTER 48

JOURNAL ENTRY

Tonight, I found out that a very close and dear childhood friend was just shot. I am beside myself with grief, I can't even process the entire situation. He was watching a sports game and one of the guests at the house starting shooting. Eddie was almost at the door when he took two bullets to the back. Several other people were injured, and there is one girl in a coma. I can't stop seeing him running around in a diaper as a toddler holding up a sucker and saying, "you can't catch me!" We spoke all the time and I don't know where to turn for support as my heart breaks. I feel like my heart is bleeding and I am completely devastated, but the astronomical pain I feel lets me know I am still alive. Life is such an uncertain thing and tomorrow is never guaranteed, you could be kissing your husband goodbye for a quick trip to the market and get in a bad wreck that snuffs you out. Or you could be out walking your dog and some hoodlum runs up and stabs you hoping to get a few bucks for his next fix. You never know when your time is up, so you have to really enjoy life and the time you have.

God I will surely miss Eddie and cherish him as I do all my lost loved ones, but I am so thankful to be alive and healthy. I am thankful to have a family who loves me and friends who care.

CHAPTER 49

JOURNAL ENTRY

A few days after Eddie's funeral Jason called me. I would have normally been surprised to get a call from one of Corey's friends, but Jason and I really started to build a friendship of our own over that year and few weeks wasted with Corey. We spent all night talking and laughing and I felt better when we ended our call. He really offered me words of comfort and I knew he was right. Eddie would not want me to be sad, he would want me to keep living and finding my joy.

I am going to go hang out with Jason at his house later on. I am going to bring the movies and popcorn and he is going to supply the beer. It will be nice to see Jason again, it has been two months since I last saw or even heard from him.

Well I had better go catch a nap before I head out

to Jason's but before I do…

"Thank you, God, for helping through the pain by giving me the understanding that you are probably hurting just as much as I am right now. The pain felt from the bloodshed, the darkness brought onto innocent people by another. I know it was never your will to allow anyone to take the life of another."

CHAPTER 50

LOST IN LUST

When I got to Jason's house, I felt happy to see him. He picked me up in a big bear hug and although my feet were dangling below me, his big arms were a welcomed shelter of friendly love. He smelled like the Nag Champa incense his was burning inside and as he put me back down, the look on his face told me he was as happy to see me as I was to see him. We settled down inside, popped a film on and had a few drinks. When the movie was over, we nursed our drinks and talked for hours. At some point we ended up in his bed enjoying each other and I felt a peaceful calm wash over me. He was gentle and concerned about what I was comfortable with. There were no serious fireworks for me because I still had walls up around my heart, but I still let myself get lost in the moment. After over an hour and both of us satisfied, I fell asleep while he worked on some music.

It wasn't long after that first night of sexual gratification, that Jason and I started to see more and more of each other. I started helping him out when he was short on cash here and there. Never in a million year did I suspect he was using meth.

A few months into us seeing each other and sleeping together, I started to notice how paranoid he was acting. Later that night after we had exhausted ourselves having sex; he grabbed his pants to get dressed, and a little bag fell out of his pocket. I picked it up and asked him what the hell was going on. At first, he tried to lie and tell me he was just holding it for a friend. I am sure the look on my face told him, I wasn't that stupid and I wasn't about to fall for that. He said he was sorry and told me the truth, he was using meth because it helped him stay focused. So, all the times I had paid his phone bill, or sold something that I held dear or went without something I needed, because I thought he would end up homeless with his cat; it was all a lie. He just needed to make sure he had enough money for his drug habit. I didn't want him to see how upset I was, so I went home and sent him a text telling him I would see him later.

I let a week go by before I saw Jason again. When I got out of my car, the way he said, "Hey mama!" then kissed my forehead made me melt. I knew that no matter how disappointed I was, he had me hooked. "Was I falling in love with him? Or was just addicted to the D and this was just lust?" I let my mind try to figure it out as I followed Jason inside, because the only thing I knew for sure was that, I couldn't stop having sex with him. It was like I was a fly that kept deliberately flying into the spider's web, no matter how many times I managed to get free.

Tammy really hated Jason and she was not shy about not sugar coating anything. If she felt it or thought it, she said it. We were alike in that way, born with no filter but yet enough sense to know when to keep our mouths shut. She always let me know what she thought right from the moment I told her about Jason and I. She said, "I don't like Jason he is just another musician that lives in a studio and sleeps on mattress on the floor or a futon I am sure. You could do far better Gwen." I don't know why but the last time she said that too me, a memory flashed back to me. So, I had to share it with her; it was back when I was dancing and nearing being done with it all. I went to grab a very late meal with the girls at a mom and pop hole in the wall diner. We just threw our robes on and went in our dancing gear since we were all so tired. When we were walking out, and there was this super attractive man sitting on the bench outside reading. He looked at me and said, "You know God can see you! You don't need to show off so much skin, you can do better." I snapped back telling him, "well apparently you can see me too, and you like what you see… because you felt the need to single me out and speak to me." Then I winked at him and kept walking to the car. It was all so strange why did that flash back to me at that moment I wondered, but quickly I shook it off. I told Tammy she needed to relax, that I could really be falling in love with Jason and that made her even more upset. She insisted that I talk to her co-worker and had him request me on myspace and Facebook.

CHAPTER 51

THE WOLF IN SHEEPS CLOTHING EXPOSED

I am so upset and I don't know why this keeps happening to me, Jason has been acting like such a fool. Perhaps I have some sign above my head that says. "all douche bag please report here!" Maybe I am secretly addicted to babysitting for free… Since I feel like I should be getting paid every time I see these immature Jackasses. I really thought Jason would be different but he is just like every other jerk on the planet! He won't speak… He won't speak to me in public, yet it is ok for him to fuck me and call me at all hours of the night. My heart hurts just thinking about how foolish I am. Then of course he has been sleeping with other women. Honestly, I can't even say that I am surprised, I mean he is Corey's friend. Why would I have expected him to treat me any better or even like I am a human being that matters? His behavior reminds me of the immaturity I dealt with when I was a teen. All the high school guys running around trying to collect notches in their beds, not giving two shits about the mental and emotional destruction of their actions. I am starting to believe that it isn't just me; all guys just never mature much further than that of a teen boy, with a warped since of morality.

Ok I am officially the stupidest woman on the plant. I got into a terrible accident driving in the rain to see Jason. My car is totaled and my body hurts all over. My ribs are broken, they had to remove glass from my eye and wanted to amputate my left hand five inches above the wrist joint down. It seems that laziness and greed are the powers that sway the level of medical care and compassion a human receives. Due do to the clean breaks and the floating piece of bone, that would have been easier and cheaper for sure, since I currently don't have medical insurance. Lucky for me I was in so much pain I didn't care and told the doctor, "oh really, that is your opinion? Well picture this, your dick doesn't work...it's broken we need to amputate!" He gave me a devilish sideways smile and said, "point taken." The doctor called in two other people to assist, gave me two ibuprofen and set my wrist. It took about forty-five minutes of pulling my wrist and dragging the chunk of bone to get all the bones in place. It hurt so bad, but working together they did it. I was thankful to keep my hand.

I really thought Jason would have come to visit with me, since I could not drive to him. About a month after the accident he finally did come visit me. After not hearing much from him, he called and told me he was coming to my house straight from the airport. When he arrived at my house, he was looking over his shoulder nonstop and asked me to clean up his arm. The wound on his arm looked pretty bad considering, he told me he just stumbled when getting on the plane. After I bandaged his arm, we had sex then he headed home. I again felt as if I let myself down by getting caught in his web again. What is wrong with my brain and will power? It is as if somewhere between my mind knowing I shouldn't continue with him, my will power over desire doesn't switch on to back it up. I am so strong and confident when I am just talking to him on the phone, but the moment I lay eyes on him my brain shuts down and I lose all my ability to think. The longer I allow this to go on, the closer I become to the morale of the men I use to dance for. A wolf seeking to fulfill my primal urges. That is not what I want to be

Since the night Jason came to me, since the night Jason came to me, he has not come to my house again. Instead calls and texts me wanting me to go to him. I have had to find ways of getting to him since I can't drive. Getting dropped off at his house or getting rides to the bar on Sunset. It has worn on me in many bad ways and I am pretty much done trying to keep his attention, I am too good for him anyway. So naturally, knowing what I know about the facts between Jason and I, it didn't make sense in my mind why I felt a cloud of jealousy seeing him flirt with some other woman at the bar. I mean he asked me to meet him here, which was strange since he was always trying to keep us a secret. I couldn't take it anymore so I walked up and started talking to the woman he was hitting on. Then I started kissing her with her right there in front of him. I wanted Jason to know that I didn't care, and that he wasn't going to break me. I needed to prove to him and to myself I could have whatever I wanted, I had the power and the beauty to demand all the attention in the room. I wanted him to see what he was taking a gamble on and was dangerously close to losing.

CHAPTER 52

JOURNAL ENTRY

I am finally starting to wise up! I have been trying to avoid Jason at all costs. He was just another pseudo friend and lover, and I am not even hurt by it. I am sure he will just move on with some other girl, possibly a groupie. I am so done with musicians and the whole Hollywood "scene" it is just a toxic pool of negativity. Everyone working in the industry tears down and damages those around them, feeding on the energy of the scared and damaged like a vampire feeds on blood. The drugs and parties fuel evils you could not ever imagine. The people that hold all the power forcing intoxication and sex upon the people with big dreams. Once they live in that world too long the innocent become corrupted. They start to seek the power and upper hand on those around; those that envy them. It is a vicious cycle that will never end, and I wash my hands of it.

I really just want to find the man who is perfect for me, he doesn't have to be perfect to the world just to me! For me to find real happiness and love, I am going to have to start cutting people out of my life. No not everyone, just the people who can't stop, with the bad choices and negativity. The people who can't seem to figure out how to behave like human beings, can't seem to figure out how to behave like human beings. The people who take and take leaving you drained of all emotion and anything else you had to offer, because they never give even an ounce back. I am starting to consider just talking to the guy that Tammy wants me to. Or, maybe I will just try to go with the flow, to finish school and my internship before I worry about meeting anyone. I wish I had a more solid plan, but it just feels better to let it all go for a while.

I am so thankful that things seem to be getting clearer for me. It seems like God is really starting to stand by me and lead me toward the right path. My mind doesn't seem as clouded and I am complaining a lot less. In my observational opinion, if you get in the habit of complaining you just end up with more things to complain about.

CHAPTER 53

LOVE MAGIC

I have caved and started talking to the co-worker of Tammy's on myspace and Facebook. Elijah is super cute in all of his photos and so funny whenever we chat. Plus I recognized him as the guy on the bench that night, the one that warned me about God watching me. We talked everyday online for two weeks, then I gave him my phone number. Now we have been talking on the phone every day.

He texts me every morning with a sweet message. I loved how he made me feel so beautiful and giddy, he made me feel a genuine happiness. We laugh and talk about everything. He is a man of God and doesn't believe in sex before marriage. I laughed so hard when he told me this and told him I didn't believe in buying the car without test driving the stick. I was only half kidding, because I would be lying if I said he didn't spark my sexual curiosity and desires. Nothing was off limits for discussion between us and it was nice to talk to a normal man for once. We were quickly becoming great friends.

A month into just talking on the phone we starting hanging out together. Elijah was so handsome and every time I was around him, I was in awe of how attractive he was. His long hair, great smile, fit body and great personality were the perfect package. I was happy to have such an amazing friend. But I was also frustrated that he didn't believe in sex before marriage because being that we were friends meant there would never be any chance of it; and I was sure I wasn't good enough for him. I called Tammy after the first time Elijah and I hung out and said, "Not funny, I am going to kill you girl!" She laughed and said," Oh you saw Elijah!" We laughed and talked about how amazing he is. She also told me how when she was chatting with me online at work, he saw my photo and asked about me. I didn't believe her, there was no way. She had to have just been really trying to push us together by making me believe that.

I have been ignoring Jason's calls for weeks and couldn't careless to be used anymore, by him or any other human being with a cock. I was focused on friends and healing from the accident. I was so close to being done with school and my perspectives and self-love were growing and changing; even faster now that I have Elijah as my friend. He really always sees things in a much better light than I ever have, and I am learning to do it to.

Elijah came over to stay the night since we would be having a few drinks while watching movies. I made a complete fool of myself after having to many drinks, I fell off the back porch and it was so funny, even if I do feel like a complete idiot. Elijah helped me up and then when we came in the house, he took me by surprise grabbing my face so gently and kissing me. I was shocked because I thought he was not interested in me at all in a romantic way, but I let myself melt into his kiss and his arms. It was the most amazing kiss I ever had in my life and the connection I felt to him was real. He smelled so manly and the feeling of being in his arms was like being held in the gentle but fiercely protective arms of an angel. I was really happy kissing him, my heart has never fluttered so fast kissing anyone, I felt fireworks and it was magical. He helped me to bed and I fell asleep shortly after that Elijah being the perfect gentlemen slept on the floor. I can't believe how sweet and respectful he is.

In the morning I got up and brushed my teeth; when I came back to the room, I told Elijah to come curl up with me and he did. It was perfect in every way and I felt the comfort and security of feeling at home in his arms. He kept calling me his future baby mama and telling me how blessed he felt and I thanked God too. This time when I thanked God it was different, I really felt thankful and happy; I knew something in me shifted for the better. I could see the person in front of me and really feel his genuine intentions. I had found a new perspective on life and I had him to thank for helping me see it. We laid in each other's arms laughing and kissing while we joked and talked; I was deeply thankful for the man next to me. I was thankful for the happiness in my heart and the genuine feelings of care between us.

That morning Elijah and I made love. It wasn't just sex and I didn't feel like a piece of meat being used as a fuck toy. It was tender and passionate and the fire between us was undeniable. I was so happy under him and in his arms, feeling him close to me, his body on mine, his soft lips kissing my lips and breasts. Feeling him gently filling me up as our bodies moved together intertwined in giving and receiving, the love we were sharing with each other. It was all so magical, better than anything I have ever experienced before, I wanted to live in this moment forever.

CHAPTER 54

JOURNAL ENTRY

I don't know why I am not writing as often as I used to, but I am trying to get something written every day. I have been doing pretty good at keeping that promise to myself too. It is just that I get so swept up having fun and laughing with Elijah, it slips my mind from time to time. I am so thankful that I have him in my life. I am even more thankful that Tammy pushed me so hard in the right direction. Without her persistence I could have missed out on an amazing love.

I never thought I could love someone so much but I love Elijah to the moon and back, he is just so perfect in every way. And the way he looks at me, like he is really seeing me with love and adoration. He just makes me so speechless sometimes and all I can do is smile because I am so happy. I have really fallen in love with

Elijah and I am so thankful God brought him into my life. I am thankful that I am so happy. I am thankful to know Elijah loves me too, it is never a question. Sometimes I pinch myself to just be sure I am not dreaming. God has really come back into my life in a big way and it may be, because Elijah helps me understand myself and my own journey with God on a deeper level. I am just beyond happy and beyond thankful.

Life has just really turned around and I am facing the right way. Now instead of falling deeper into the rabbit hole, I am walking the surface in light with God at my side. I have a better perspective and understanding as to how to keep myself and those around me happy. Thank You God!

CHAPTER 55

ELIJAH

It wasn't long before Elijah was living with me at my parent's house. We wanted to save for a place of our own and we couldn't stay with his mother, she hated me. She depended on him so much, it was as if I stole her husband away from her. She even tried to run me over with her car when she saw us leaving her house. I was completely shaken by her behavior and quickly learned that she was not ok with me at all, because she planned for her oldest son to watch his siblings and contribute to bills. She even shut his phone off and then would sit up calling mine at all hours of the night. This went on until she just accepted that we loved each other and wanted to be together.

Elijah and I never fight or argue and life is total bliss. He is working helping people and I just landed a job with the FBI. Normally it would have taken longer, but with my course grades and test scores being so high, I got in with the help of a family friend at the top. I was excited that strings were pulled to get me in so fast, I couldn't wait to start saving people and catching bad guys. I had spent so long being a victim in my own life, I was finally ready to be on the flip side of the coin. I am so thankful for Elijah because he shared his beliefs in gratitude and positivity. It is still a weak muscle for me but I am working at it every day and it is paying off. The more positive my perspective remains, the happier I become. I wish I would have been taught to practice this all my life, but most of the world is taught to gripe and complain. Rather than being thankful for what they do have, they bitch and moan about what they don't. Like a magnet whatever you project out you get back. The positive, thankful vibes and words have really turned my life around. I owe all my new-found thoughts, words and positivity skills to Elijah. We are truly meant to be.

CHAPTER 56

JOURNAL ENTRY

Life has really been better than I ever imagined it could be. I was lucky enough and brave enough to do the hardest internships to get me a job right out of school. Working in the psychiatric ward alongside some of the best physiatrists in the business was a challenge at first, but it quickly became easy and so exciting. Learning how to read behaviors and learning what makes people tick was so interesting. I am glad that I chose out of three options offered to me, to have my specialty as a profiler to have my specialty as a profiler. Sure, because I wanted work right out of college, I had to take a secondary internship working alongside an FBI behavioral analysis team; to observe and offer insight when I saw it. I am glad that my instructor for abnormal psychology, a retired FBI BAU agent believed enough in me to write a letter of recommendation and made that internship happen for me. Without it, I don't know if they would have accepted me on the team; even with strings being pulled.

Things between Elijah and I have been amazing, he is amazing. I am so deeply in love with him. He is always pushing me with encouragement to meet my goals and make my dreams a reality. Things with his mother have smoothed over somewhat and we are just living happily together, banking every penny we can. We are planning on buying a house soon; if only we find one that we love and manage to have saved enough for the home we fall in love with. I am sure everything will be work out, because with God and gratitude all things are possible.

CHAPTER 57

THE PROPOSAL

I am so happy, Elijah took me out to dinner to celebrate our love and happiness and then... he proposed! It was so romantic, we had a quiet dinner in a booth at Black Angus. I know he chose that restaurant because they have the booths that create privacy. We just talked about everything that was going on in life for us and how grateful we were for each other. We talked about all the achievements and goals we have to meet, both together as a couple and as individuals. Then we went for a walk on the beach and he wrapped a blanket around me, he took from the back seat of the car. Then he just held me while we watched the waves. I was breathing in the manly scent of his Suavage cologne, that mixed with his body chemistry and made me crave his touch even more than usual. The smell of the beach and the salty damp air surround us; the cold wet sand under my feet was all so much more perfect while I was in his arms. I would have been happy to just stay there in that moment for an eternity. Then suddenly Elijah took my hand and told me, "Gwen, I love you so much. You are so smart and beautiful, you have a kind heart and share so much love and happiness with everyone around you. You help those who can't help themselves selflessly and never complain; you make me want to be a better man each and every day. I can't imagine my life without you." Then took a ring box from his pocket and opened it as he got down on one knee and asked me to marry him. I thought I was going to die from joy. I started crying tears of happiness and thankfulness and just started saying yes over and over! Then we had a long tender kiss. It was the best night of my life.

We planned our wedding pretty quickly and got married three months later. The wedding planning was simple yet stressful, I guess I didn't realize how expensive things would get. Then when our family members started to fight with us about the close date and their conveniences, we just started whittling away at the guest list. In the end it was a small ceremony and reception with just our immediate family and closest friends. Tammy was of course my maid of honor, my only bride's maid actually. After all, without her we may have never even met, I was so thankful to her for pushing me to talk to him and introducing us via our social media accounts.

We found a house that we are in love with and I hope that everything goes smoothly in the buying process. After such a stressful wedding, I don't think I can handle anymore hiccups. Work is great and Elijah and I are enjoying married life, I couldn't have asked for a better man. I pinch myself sometimes in disbelief. I am finally happy and I love living my life with my new positive perspective. My new perspective on life and what is going on around me really helps me to see, that the best choice in how I respond. No matter what is going on in life, no matter what people say, only we can decide how we respond. I try to keep my own responses positive or internal and now I finally feel like my feet are firmly on the ground, the future is bright for me.

CHAPTER 58

WEDDED BLISS

Elijah and I have been settled into our new house for a couple of months and I couldn't be happier. We spend every second we can together, if we aren't out having fun on a date, we are at home making love. We even christen every room in the house during the unpacking process. I love being in love, there is no better feeling. It having someone you love as much as they love you and always reflecting back in one big circle to one another, is like nothing else on earth. I have been so happy working and being a wife; although for the past few days I have been feeling really sick. He has been so wonderful taking care of me, but since I don't feel any better I am getting concerned. I just feel so tired all the time and this nausea I feel seems to be getting worse.

I called my mom while Elijah was out at work, since I had the day off and I told her how I have been feeling tired and can't seem to stop vomiting but I have no fever. So, she came buy with a pregnancy test, I don't know why it never occurred to me that I could be pregnant. I guess I thought that forgetting to take one or two pills last month wouldn't have made that much of an impact on the effectiveness of the birth control. After peeing on the test, the positive result came up so fast there was no wait time. I am so excited I can't wait for Elijah to get home, I want to share the news with him face to face.

When Elijah got home from work, I had just finished cooking dinner and had started putting it on the table. He kissed me, greeting me by telling me how happy he was to come home to his lovely wife and how thankful he was to be married to his best friend. His words always seemed to bring positive thoughts to mind, "I am so thankful for him and sometimes I want to take snapshots of my life with Elijah, just to be sure I remember every cherished moment our of lives together."

Over dinner we talk about how his day was.

The selfless way he tells me about all the people he has been able to help makes me so proud of him. Then I tell him I have a gift for him, telling him it was something special that would always remind us of our love, as I hand him a gift bag. He is so surprised and asking me what the occasion, but I just told him it was simply an I love you gift. When he opened the bag and pulled out the pregnancy test, he looked confused, and asked who's it was. I laughed and told him, "mine silly!" He stood up and hugged me so tightly and tears of joy welled in his eyes. Then he kissed me and told me we could clean up the table later. He kissed me while hold me around the waist while leading me to our room. He slowly took my clothes while laying gentle kisses along my body and telling me how much he loved me. After softly and lovingly removing my panties he kissed my stomach as he climbed slowly on top of me. His eyes told me how happy he was and how much he loved me. We made love and whispered our love and joy to each other while sharing every part or our gratitude for the blessing of a baby. We spent the night making love and becoming one, letting our souls melt together as one.

Once Elijah fell asleep, I got up to clean the dinner dishes. I let all my thoughts run free, I kept asking myself how I got so lucky. What changed the way God saw me, what was I doing differently? Then I realized God didn't change the way he saw me, I changed the way I saw God. I was seeing everything around me in a new light. Instead of seeing the negative in things I saw the positive. I thanked God and the universe every day for all my blessings and now I have a wonderful husband and a baby on the way. Life is a so amazing.

CHAPTER 59

A BUNDLE OF JOY

I am eight months along with this pregnancy and it has been quite the doozey.

I have been so sick and can no longer eat some of my favorite foods, the smells just make me so sick. When I was only twenty-five weeks along hyperemesis really threatened to take my baby from me. Elijah couldn't be there with me because he was on a business trip and couldn't find a flight home in time. I know he wanted to be there with me. My mom was so great, she stayed with me the entire time, since Elijah couldn't make it. I was glad the hospital staff was so quick at getting the contractions to stop. Forty-eight long hours later I was finally allowed to go home. I was glad to be back home because I was in full nesting mode.

The closer I get to my due date the stronger my

need to "nest" becomes as I make everything ready for the baby; and now that I am only four short weeks away from my due date, I can't stop over thinking. I clean and rearrange and then do it all over again. I was glad that Elijah was able to put all the baby furniture together, so I could get everything just where I want it in the nursery. Only I have been feeling contractions all day, but then again maybe they are just braxton hicks and I should put it in the back of my mind.

A few hours after getting settled into bed I notice my contractions are really strong and I can't ignore them. They are about thirty minutes apart but still something doesn't feel right. These contractions feel different, I feel like I need to hold my breath through them and I can't move. Elijah takes me to the hospital and everyone in the labor and delivery unit seems to be acting as if there isn't a worry. When the doctor enters the room, he tells me that when the nurse checked me when I came in, I was one centimeter dilated and now three hours later there was no change. He says not worry about the contractions but to drink more water to help ease them. Then he tells us to make sure we address any concerns with our doctor, the following Thursday at our appointment. I am worried but Elijah helps calm me down and we go home and lay in bed while he sings to the baby and I start to melt into relaxation. Listening to him sing and talk to the baby tugs at my heart strings. I watch our baby respond to the sound of daddy's voice and as my stomach moves around Elijah kisses it. I am so thankful for this moment. I am in awe at the power and miracle my body has provided this far, my body has grown a tiny human being inside it. A tiny human that is half Elijah and half me is waiting to emerge into the world; then a sudden moment of fear falls upon me. "What if I can't do this what if I am a bad mom? How does someone teach a baby to talk or walk?" As soon as the thoughts flood my head Elijah grabs my hand and I know it will all be ok.

As these past two weeks have moved along fast and so have my contractions. They just seem to roll on into the following day and never seem to go away. It doesn't matter how much water I drink or how calm I try to stay, they just won't stop. I am glad that we have another doctor's appointment in two days, by then I will be thirty-nine weeks exactly. Elijah has been wonderful and helps me walk off the pain, I couldn't have found a better more loving and supportive man. He never drops the ball and never disappoints me.

The morning of our doctor's appointment Elijah and I wake up really early and we make love. The pain I feel while we are lost in the throes of love becomes so intense, that we have to stop because am not sure it is anything too serious. Elijah helps me get cleaned up in the shower and get dressed, because I am almost doubling over in pain.

Once we sit down with our doctor and I explain what is going on, the doctor checks me and I am at three centimeters. He sends me over for induction because my contracts are still thirty minutes apart. When we walk into the labor and delivery room I am taken over by nerves and I get goosebumps. I decide to pee before putting on the hospital gown I was given; even though as soon I change, I will have to pee again. I head into the bathroom as Elijah tells me he will return with some ice for me and coffee for himself. When I am done going pee, I find myself stuck on the toilet in a wave of pain. Since Elijah went down to get coffee the nurse helps me up and gets me settled into the hospital bed. Once Elijah is back, I feel ready to have this baby, I am sick of being in pain and I feel brave with him at my side.

Eighteen very long and painful hours of labor later andI am not moving along as a they would like; so the next step is to break my water. Once the doctor breaks my water the contractions become closer and stronger than ever. The nurse calls the anesthesiologist and he come with a resident in tow. The resident does my epidural and when she is finished, I suddenly feel like I have to go to the bathroom. Everyone looks at each other which tells me that is not as good sign or at least not how they planned for this to happen. The nurse comes over to check me and says she can feel the baby's head. She tells me not to push because she has to page the doctor on call, but the urge is just too much. I can feel every inch of my vagina stretching and tearing, since I didn't get the epidural in time. I try to ignore the fact that I feel every bit of pain that childbirth has for me, and just focus on the fact that soon I will be holding my baby in my arms.

After five minutes of pushing I have my baby on my chest. Elijah is kissing me, telling how wonderful I did and how beautiful our new son is. But while Elijah cuts the cord the nurses take my baby and start working on him. His leg can't seem to stay a healthy pink, so they are shouting out facts, like… his cord wasn't wrapped and his vitals as they rush him to the NICU. I am so scared and there is nothing I can do, so Elijah follows our baby to the hospital NICU while I stay back and get stitches. The doctor tries to comfort me with words as he sews up the tear I now have from my vagina to my asshole. His words don't help because I can't think about anything more than my baby.

After three long hours of praying and crying, I get my baby back. The nurses tell me that it was most likely a complication from being in active labor so long. The constant contractions disrupted his circulation. I am so thankful to hold my baby and I am grateful to the nurses for saving his leg. As I hold my baby the rest of the world falls away.

When I sit up to nurse my new bundle of joy, I have a sudden headache that is so bad I would rather experience natural childbirth one hundred times back to back, than take this pain for a second longer. So, I lay back down and the nurses put the baby to my breast. I have a spinal headache, I am going to need a blood patch and to stay on my back for three days. How am I going to do that with a new born?

One full week after delivery, the baby and I are finally home and I am thankful. Elijah and I can start to enjoy our new little family. He has been so amazing helping with diapers and doing whatever he can; aside from feeding because baby and I are exclusively nursing. Life is so full and I don't know what could possibly make it better.

CHAPTER 60

JOURNAL ENTRY

The months are just flying by. The baby is growing like a weed and I can't stop calling him the baby or just baby. Not that I don't love the name Elijah and I chose, Gavin is suited perfectly for him and it will work well when he is man. The baby stage is so short, and I am trying to enjoy every second of it. I have been back to work for a few weeks now and pumping has really been a challenge at times. It isn't exactly like I can take a time out while working a case to pump. All in all I have managed fairly well.

When I am with my baby holding him in my arms, I just feel so blessed. There is so much love in his eyes when he looks at me, and the way he smiles at me when I am nursing him makes me giggle with joy and love. I love him more than I love anyone and I will do whatever it takes to keep him safe and provide for him. His little hands always gripping my fingers remind me just how much he needs me and I need him, this little person is more than I could have ever hoped for he is the physical proof and result of the love between me and Elijah.

I was so foolish for blaming God for so many years, for all the wrongs in my life. I was so busy complaining and being jealous, or so confused I couldn't see I had another choice in every situation. I missed the signals that God put there for me to see, because I was too negative to see anything that was actually bad for me. I surrounded myself with like-minded people that stay lost, blinded for too long. Nothing that happened to me had anything to do with God. It was all me.

My actions caused a reaction, my words mattered because like the energy of them being push from my thoughts and mind, they clung to like energies that boomeranged back to me. I was getting in my own way. Every time I blamed God or others it was all pulling more negativity and evil into my life. As soon as I started seeing the positive in every situation and being thankful, life got better. Instead of hating the negative people around me, I started asking God to bless them and help them, and it drove my life rapidly to happiness.

At this stage in my life I have a wonderful husband and a beautiful baby and I look forward to the future. Even work isn't ever something I see in a negative light I don't look at the people I track down as evil, they are just lost and broken. Like everyone else they haven't found out how to be happy and hurting others, dragging them down makes them feel empowered. It is the ultimate form of complaining and jealousy, to snuff out the light in someone you want or can't have, someone who seems better off than you are... It all boils down to one thing... perspective!

CHAPTER 61

AND BABY MAKES FOUR

Well nine months after our first baby was born, we found out we were expecting a second baby. It was a blessing beyond stars; but the fear of two babies in diapers and two babies so close in age got to me at first. But like always Elijah is just happy and so thankful, he helps put me at ease and that helps me see I am thankful too.

I have been just as sick as I was through the first pregnancy. Only this time, the pain I am having in my hips is because I am over producing the hormones that help the body during labor and delivery. The pain and stress on my body was so much, I had to be put on bed rest which I am not happy about. I have a baby to take care of so it just isn't ideal to be on bed rest. Then to top it off, at the first anatomy ultrasound appointment yesterday the ultrasound tech put the towel across my stomach and told me she would be back. I thought she had to pee or something simple, but when she came in with the doctor, I became so worried. I knew something wasn't right, laying there watching them search my baby over and over. "What are they looking for?" Then after the longest ten minutes of my life the doctor looks at me and says well, I have good news and bad news. My heart sank to the pit of my stomach. She then says good news is, it's a boy; bad news is, I can't see his stomach. I tuned the doctor out after those words, all I could hear was the pulsing of the blood in my body and I felt as if I was caught underwater.

Elijah had to pretty much carry me out of the office I was in such a state of shock. I could not stop the flood of thoughts crowding my mind. "Was it something I did wrong? What would have caused that?" I just stared out of the window and cried until we got home. Elijah helped me lay down and cuddled me until I fell asleep, I think he knew I was not ready to talk or listen.

Later when I woke up, I saw that my mom had brought my sweet little man home and it helped ease the pain of what I just dealt with. Elijah came over and sat down with me taking my hand. He explained everything, he knew I tuned out earlier. He told me that the doctor is going to continue to scans every week until they can see what is going on, because the issue is so rare and is mostly always only seen with dwarfism. He said they are pretty sure dwarfism isn't the case. So, I tried to calm down and put it out of my mind.

But week after week they couldn't find his stomach. Added to my stress the baby had decreased fetal movement. Due to the concern for the health of the baby and his drop-in activity the doctor had me go to fetal diagnostic every other day. I wasn't sure if I could handle much more. I was struggling to pray and remain positive, it was all I had to cling to. So, I forced myself to picture my arms holding my happy, healthy baby and I was able to be thankful for the baby growing in my womb.

At thirty-three weeks pregnant I walked into my doctor's appointment and just broke down. He said aside from the fetal movement monitoring he was unaware of the other issue as the ultrasound facility had not notified him of it. So, he had me lay down and he got the ultrasound machine out, when he touched it to my pregnant belly... he found my son's stomach in a matter of seconds. I felt a wave a joy and relief wash over me and I was over the moon. All of my prayers and gratitude had paid off.

CHAPTER 62

JOURNAL ENTRY

With a week before the baby is due to arrive, my mother-in-law has lost her ever loving mind. She really thinks I should let her be in the delivery room, is she insane? I am going to be spread eagle pushing a human out of my body, unless you put the baby there or you are taking it out you are not in the delivery room! She has been causing so many arguments between Elijah and I. She is always lurking around listening for an opening to attack me; it is really stressful. I told her she could watch Gavin while we went to deliver our new arrival. She still wasn't happy, she always feels she should be included but this is a private intimate moment for us as a couple. We made the baby that way and the baby should come into the world that way.

I know I need to work harder on my gratitude and

positivity and that it seems like I am a ranting raging bitch, but this is only because I am a pregnant hormonal raging bitch. My mother in-law is not making it any easier on me either. I want to pray that the Lord bless her and help her but I will admit there are times when she makes it too damn difficult. What does she expect from me, I am only human just like everyone else. I wish she would back off and let Elijah and I be happy. I wish she would be supportive and respectful of our wishes.

CHAPTER 63

JOURNAL ENTRY

I am glad I picked up my journal on the way out the hospital for my fetal diagnostics appointment. I did not expect to go into labor or for it to progress so quickly. I was expecting to have a least a little time to labor at home, but after two hours my contractions had dropped from every thirty minutes apart to every fifteen. Then over the next hour the contractions dropped again to seven minutes, so we didn't have time to circle back to the house after dropping Gavin off with Elijah's mom. By the time I was in the hospital room my labor was threatening to stall, but I was nearly fully dilated and I wasn't going to accept that. I was determined to have a natural child birth this time. I wanted to have the least amount of intrusion while Elijah and I welcomed our second child. After six big pushes baby Timothy joined the world, and all the love and joy I felt for my first baby, I felt equally for my second baby.

The baby came a week early and I had no spinal headache because I declined the epidural. I was able to get up and shower and pee right after giving birth, which was nice. The next day the baby and I were sent home and I was happy to be with my family at home. It was a real miracle that the baby and I got through pregnancy and delivery healthy after all the worry that we endured.

CHAPTER 64

PURE LOVE

I am currently sitting in the hospital nursing my ten-day old new born and crying. He hasn't been able to poop since I brought him home and he spits up everything he takes in. I am so worried there is something seriously wrong. The hospital is admitting him and I am a mess, I need to focus. The problem is, all I seem to focus on is how rough the pregnancy I had with him was and the trouble they had locating his stomach. I can't help but wondering if something was over looked. As the tears fall down my face, I kiss his bald little head and pray.

My baby turned blue and wasn't breathing and I had to do CPR on him until the nurses ran in. He started spiting up and just went blue. I have never been so afraid. I watched in horror as they worked on him, and did the only thing I had in my power to do, I prayed. The tears streaming down my face a reminder that this was not a nightmare, I was living this. I was fighting with negative thoughts and the what if's in my mind, and just tried to focus on how blessed I am to have my children. How thankful I was to God for helping my baby and providing him with a body that is always healing and a spirit that is always fighting. I let those thoughts play in my focused mind over and over, then suddenly the color flushes back into his little body. They put oxygen on my tiny infant and some other monitors and order some tests. After days of tests and many doctors I find out he has GURD which is extreme acid reflux. So, the internist puts him on some medication to help him keep his feedings down and digest. A couple of days later and we are home again.

The medication worked so well that at nine months old he was pulled off of it. Now as I watch my two boys play while sitting next to Elijah, I am reminded about the power of my prayers. I am reminded that my words, thoughts and prayers matter and they can drive your life to go in one direction or another. I have a great career, a wonderful family that lives in a home full of love. I escaped all the tainted deceptions that tried to drag me down, by pretending to be love and I found the real thing. I am so thankful for everything that has happened in my life good or bad because it is why I am the woman I am today. They are the events that put me right where I needed to be and led me to my husband, who gave me my kids. Everything that impacted me; it's all etched into me and although some of those things were negative the positive things, I allow to be implanted deeper into my being. I purge the negative and give it to God, I forgive those who wrong me and pray for the Lord to bless them and help them. I forgive them for me, and give their wrongs committed against me, to God, for God. It is not my place to judge them or feel anger toward them that is for the Lord. For all these reasons I am happy choosing to be a wife and a mother, because with God at my side, gratitude in my heart and positivity in my mind... I can do whatever I put my mind to.

CHAPTER 65

STARING MY PAST IN THE FACE

For the past two years things have been great, life just has an easy flow to it. Elijah and I have settled into and nice flow of work and family. We have found the perfect balance and I am thankful for that. I think about how far I have come in life and how happy life is as I walk into work.

I walk into my office to file the paperwork from the case my team and I just solved, as one of my team members John walks into my office. His face has an expression of both concern and anxiety as he tells me we have a new case; the police found another body. The murder victim is a blonde stripper known for prostitution. I grab my work issue cell and follow John to the car.

On the ride over to the murder scene John gives me all the details he knows. The victim was found in an alley in North Hollywood, she is blonde haired, blue eyed and is an ex-stripper turned prostitute. The body was discovered by tenants of the apartment complex that line the alley. The body was clothed and cut open from the vagina to the sternum, leaving her disemboweled. The ring finger of the left hand was cut off and has yet to be located. As I am hearing the details, I try not to let myself flash back to the past because I know that the police have stated they think we are dealing with a copycat murderer.

When we arrive on the scene, I clear all thoughts from my mind. I have to approach every scene and every new crime without bias, or suggestions that may cloud what I am seeing. When I walk over and kneel beside the body, I see her face and immediately recognize her; it's Melissa. Just as the realization of who the victim laying in the pool of blood before me, has hit me; John pulls me aside, he said, "Gwen, you are gonna want to see this!"

"See what, and have we spoken to the people who found the body yet?"

"The police have found the victims bag in the dumpster, and there is disc with your name on it."

"Well let's have these guys take photos, I want the dumpster lid printed and possible witnesses questioned, so have some uniforms start door knocking. Let's go to the station and get that disc to analysis and find out what is on it."

Racing back to the station with my partner while the rest of our team stayed back to collect more intel, I was wondering what was going on. I told my partner that I recognized the victim from my childhood, and he addressed the same concern I had. What was on that disc and what did it have to do with me.

Once the analysis team viewed the disc and they logged it into evidence. They played the footage for my partner, myself and detective Lopez, who invited us onto the case. It was the killer documenting the torture and murder of Melissa. This guy was toying with me, but why?

As the team regrouped in the conference room with the local law enforcement, we compiled the known similar cases to compare. I didn't believe this was just another copycat. I had the team pull the details from Natalie Brown's AKA "Persway's" murder case to follow up on the details and any leads that had gone cold. This killer was not going to allude me, I won't allow it.

When my boss hears how personally close this case it to me, he tries to bench me. He didn't want me to personalize or miss things because it was so close to me. It wasn't close to me these were people in my past, a past I let go of long ago, besides it didn't matter; he knows I am damn good at what I do and my team is compiled of the best of the best. I know we will catch this sick fucker and I know the team can't do it without me. My obsessive compulsive attention to detail and memory is vital as well as my ability to read people and the situations around me. My past is what trained me and prepared me for this job, it doesn't define me.

I just hope I catch him before he kills again…

Escaping Tainted Love